# THE DIARY OF ZARTOON

## By R.e. Taylor

© 2014 **Shadowlight** Books
Brisbane, Queensland, Australia

# Dedication

When I was a boy I saw a TV show that took me on a journey through this quadrant of the galaxy. Gene Roddenberry created that show. It was called Star Trek and it got my young mind interested in the limitless possibilities of science fiction. Later Carl Sagan turned me onto the true science of the universe. This story is dedicated to the two of them and their hopes for mankind and the universe we all live in.

R.e.

## ENTRY 1
27.02.63.28.15

I do not know what happened. One minute I was in Elkston, Maine, and the next minute I am on the side of some ravine in some, god forsaken desert. There are a few plants nearby, but their leaves are a deep red. I was always taught not to eat red plants, they could poison you... so, despite feeling really hungry, all I can do is sit here and look at those red plants.

You know, this is madness, what is going on? What has happened to me? I had better check to make sure I'm okay and not hurt. Maybe I have bashed my head and am hallucinating or something. No, There is not a mark on me, my arms, legs and all my body parts seem to be in perfect working order. There is a slight scratch that runs the length of my forearm, but it is not that bad. I guess I'll make it!

I found this notebook and pen in my jacket, so to help stop me from feeling that I am going utterly insane, I am going to write down my thoughts.

There are some footprints on the floor of the ravine. I can't make out what they are but they aren't that big. I think whatever it is, it walks on four legs and isn't moving very fast. I should be able to catch it.

It is now a few hours later, or at least I think it is a few hours later. I did manage to catch the creature causing the footprints. It was just a rodent, about the size of one of those vermin I used to hunt back home.

I tried cooking it, but for some reason, every time I tried lighting a match it just flashed and went out. Went out... my ass! It never got close to lighting so I ended up eating the damn rodent raw.

The sun had just gone down, and I could never believe that there were so many stars in the sky. They were all so beautiful, but one in particular caught my attention. It was a bright blue star that hugged the horizon for about twenty minutes before it sank down behind a mountain that was many miles away across the ravine.

I am now feeling extremely tired, I have to sleep, so goodnight where ever I am, and hopefully I'll still be alive in the morning.

## ENTRY 2
28.02.63.18.08

The sun came up about an hour ago. It is not bright at all, and even in the late morning the sky still looks like sunset. There are no clouds to speak of and the shadows of the rocks are so clear I can't believe what I am seeing. But, there in the distance, is a very, very faint line of red mist in the sky.

I know that, although I have shelter, I am going to have to go out of this little cave. I need to find water and some place where there is more than just one rodent to eat. I have to keep my body working until I can find out where I am and how I got here.

Later: I climbed down the rocks and started heading to where that mist was. Maybe I was seeing things... a reflection from the sun hitting the sky... or the mist could have been real. I know that I was hungry and very thirsty, so maybe that could be affecting my mind, but surely I did get enough nourishment from the rodent to last a little while. No, I don't think that this is all in my head, but still, maybe a doctor would have a different opinion.

I have been walking for a couple of hours now. My cave is just a distant memory. I looked back a little bit ago and I couldn't even see the hill where the cave was. Everything around me was just flat. Suddenly, like some sort of flash, a memory came back. I had taken a trip from New York City to San Diego. I remember I passed through Oklahoma on the way and I swear that I could have seen Canada from where we were. It, and this new land, is also just that flat. Strange how that flash memory from my past suddenly came to me. I only wish I really knew who I was and where I actually belonged. Who was I, what did I do in life, who did I even love? None of that I could remember. Sadly, I knew I must accept this fact if I was to survive, but let me tell you I did not like it at all.

The sun is directly above me, but the air is cold. Am I in winter? I did notice some scars in the soil. There were once rivers that flowed here. Going by the size of them, it was about the width of the Niagara River but not nearly as deep. They looked like they were maybe a meter or two deep and there were some marks in the valleys that showed that, at one time, it was a raging river carrying huge rocks and debris with it. God, I wish there was still water flowing here. It would have cured my thirst, and also had some fish in it that I could have eaten.

"Wait a minute," I said to myself, "I must be some kind of freaking idiot." I remember the Boy Scouts and what they taught us. In a river bed, dig down and you may find water!!! I thought for a minute and then I moved down and start digging. The scouts were right. There was water. It was rusty and smelt like a pile of dog shit, but I had to have it or I knew I would die for sure.

The water tasted as bad as it smelled, but I drank it, and even washed in it, and then I lay down to get some rest and maybe sleep through the night. All I can think of right now is what the hell am I doing here?

# ENTRY 3
## 01.03.63.42.18

Again, I was up with the sun. I wasn't thirsty, but I could hear the sounds of my stomach. They were loud enough to block out the sounds of the winds.

The mist I saw the day before was still there. It didn't look any closer, but at least I had a target to aim for. I walked about ten miles and I saw something amazing... the ground was still reddish and dry as hell, but on some of the rocks I saw something green. It wasn't a lot, but it was there. Kneeling down to look at it, I had seen this before. I knew I had. It was a moss, I had seen it growing in between the cracks of a broken sidewalk. (I wonder where? Oh, why can't I remember, this is crazy!)

Taking a small piece I licked it with my tongue. It tasted sweet! Almost as sweet as perfectly ripe cantaloupe, but it had a musky scent to it. Grabbing bigger and bigger chunks I swallowed them down without chewing them. It wasn't long before I was full, and I started walking again.

Having eaten, I had my strength back, so I started climbing a mountain that was a few hundred yards away. It took me all day to reach the top. The thing was... the higher I climbed, the warmer the air began feeling, until it was more than comfortable for me.

I have found a crack in one of the massive stones, and am writing this next entry and then I hope to get some sleep... but before I do, I can't help but look up at that blue star in the sky... I don't know why I am drawn to it, but I've been watching it for about an hour now, it is so beautiful. My eyes are starting to close, I think it is time I went to sleep. Maybe, I will wake up in the morning and find this was all a dream, or maybe that this is my hell and I am the only human alive on this strange planet.

## ENTRY 4
03.03.63.01.34

I cannot believe that I have been asleep for a day and a half. I know this as I am wearing a watch which tells the time and date. I know nothing about why I am wearing this watch, did I buy it, did someone give it to me? All I know is, I am wearing it, so it must be mine. It was good to sleep like that, it must have been the warmth and that I had had something to eat that made me relax so much. I cannot believe how many stars are out. I may just be able to see the entire universe from here, but I know that is impossible. I can't even see the whole galaxy. Who really cares! It's beautiful! The horizon is a beautiful shade of dark, dark orange. There is something there that I hadn't seen yet... there were two moons rising. I have got to say that was quite a shock to say the least. "Where did that second moon come from?" I asked myself not knowing if I was seeing what I was seeing or if my mind finally started to go.

I thought about it for a minute. Then I turned and faced the direction I was traveling before. That mist was still there. I could still see it despite the darkness. I felt funny looking at it... It was almost as if whatever it is, or was... it was calling me to it.

I started down the trail when I heard water running. It wasn't the kind of sound you'd expect from a shower or bath. It was more like the kind of sound water makes when it rolls down a drainpipe. The sound wasn't coming from far away so I stopped and looked around. There, between two red rocks, was a small creek flowing down the hill. I will tell you... my mouth started watering at the thought of finally finding some fresh flowing water. But, to make the day, even a bit brighter there were tiny fish swimming around one of the pools. They weren't big in any sense of the word... maybe just an inch and a half, but there were thousands of them and I was so hungry. I grabbed up a couple of handfuls of the fish and gulped them down without any effort.

Full and rested, I sat and looked into the valley. The moons had long since set behind one of the mountains and the sun was coming up. Strangely, the sky was not the red that it had been the last few days. Rather, it was a faint violet, turning blue as you looked in the direction I was walking in.

I saw some straight black lines crossing the valley. There was little else but rocks and a few cracks but those lines... they were strange and caught my attention. So I slightly changed my direction and headed for the closest of the lines, which was still further away than it looked. It took me the rest of the day to cover, God, I don't know how many miles, but I finally made it and it looked just as strange as it did from on top of the mountain. It was perfectly straight and looked like it went on forever.

The sun was going down so I gathered my stuff and settled down for the night along the black line. Oh well... another night in the wilderness, but this time I waited for those moons to rise so that I knew I wasn't imagining them.

## ENTRY 5
04.03.63.12.36

The air was so much clearer this morning. The mist was still there, but it was so much closer than it had been. I could see shapes hidden in the mist. They looked like spires reaching up beyond the mist and into a blue sky. I could also see some small objects flying around the area. They weren't just drifting on the breezes... they were powered, and under some kind of control, since they were making maneuvers that nothing in nature could ever make. I mean, I watched one make a 270 degree turn with barely a loss in speed.

Now this part is pure speculation, because while I was watching what was in front of me... I was knocked out from behind. I didn't see who, or what, it was that hit me, but I do know that I went down like a proverbial bag of rocks. When I woke up, I was not sure how long after I was hit, my back and my ass had burns on them and the back of my clothes were shredded. My arm felt like it was torn out of its socket, but at least I was alive.

My eyes opened and I saw creatures of some kind. They were green and about seven feet tall. Their skin was reptilian, their faces were humanoid and their eyes were large and were soft blue with large white pupils. "Tih gerk sli sitew petoq," one of them said as he knelt down to me. He was holding a cup of liquid, and he seemed friendly enough. "Tih gerk sli sitew petoq," he said again as he held the cup to his lips. Then he moved the cup close to my mouth and repeated the same words again before what I could only guess was a female, took the cup from his hand and handed it to me.

"Tih gerk sli sitew petoq," she said as she guided my hand to my lips. I took a drink, and she smiled and pointed to herself. "Tigqu yev taqi pagok," she said. Then she placed her hand on my chest and smiled again. "My name is Williams from Phoenix," I said.

She got a bigger smile and said as she pointed at my chest, "Fa Nex." I assumed that, to her, that was my name... Fa Nex. She sat down next to me and stroked my hair. "Fa Nex, uta kah legut ta," she said. She never once stopped smiling as I told her I could not understand her. She walked away for just a moment and handed me a small blue pill. "Tih gerk sli sitew peted," she said as she handed me the pill.

Well, she hadn't hurt me yet, so I took the pill and, after about 10 minutes, I could understand what she was saying, and she could understand me. "Fa Nex," she started. "You are one of those from the Human city?" I told her that I had never been to the city and I had no idea where I was.

She took a stick and drew 9 circles on the ground with a dot on each circle. Then she took the stick and pointed to the fourth circle. "You are here," she said. Then a light went on in my head. "You are on Zartoon." She had such a smile that she was so pleased with herself.

"I am on Mars." I asked.
"No," she said "Zartoon!"
I took the stick and pointed to the third circle. "I am from Earth," I said. "That planet there."

"Yartook," she said. "No, you are on Zartoon." Then it hit me. I somehow either left the Earth, or I had lost my mind, but suddenly I got really dizzy and I passed out in front of her.

## ENTRY 6
## 04.03.63.21.34

I have no idea how long I have been out. I just know that I woke up on a platform that was covered with thick furs. The female from earlier was standing next to me, as if she was watching me sleep. "Fa Nex, are you okay," she asked as she helped me from the "bed" and onto a bench that was sitting close by. I told her that I was fine and, finally, she introduced herself to me. "Fa Nex, my name is Pandorica. I am here to help you in any way I can and to show you that my people are not as bad as you have been told."

"Pandorica," I said with a smile. "I know nothing of your people or Zartoon. We were always taught that planets like yours were devoid of all life. That they were just big red dust balls."

"Fa Nex, please come with me," she said as she finished dressing me and then walked me toward the door. "We have a special meal prepared for you." she stated softly with a warm smile. I suddenly felt extremely safe in her presence; she made me feel that I was not, after all, utterly alone.

She escorted me to a big tent colored to match the surrounding desert. "Please sit here," she said as she pointed to a deep red velvet seat. Then she waved her finger and two scantily clad Human females walked over to me and fed me some of the most delicious meat I had ever had. I asked what it was, but nobody answered me, so I just continued to enjoy it even though it was a secret.

After dinner, I was escorted back to my room and as soon as I got in there one of the Human females walked in and knelt down in front of me. "Fa Nex," she said in a very soft demure voice. "I am here for your pleasure. Pandorica said that you are to be pleased and that I cannot say no to anything you wish."

I looked at her. She had a body that was so far beyond belief. But, I was not going to take advantage of her, despite all she offered, so instead we just spent the night talking. She told me that she was given shelter as a little girl and raised by the people she served. "I am not a slave," she said. "I am part of this culture and they treat me very well. I never want for anything. That is more than I can say about the Human city; it is not the same there." She told me so much about herself and Zartoon, and we kept talking for hours, until an extremely tall Zartoon male came for her.

A few minutes later, just as the sun set, Pandorica walked in and shared a drink with me. I have no idea what it was but I got sleepy, very sleepy, so I lay down on the furs and, for some reason, Pandorica lay down beside me and cuddled close and that was all I remember before I fell asleep.

I was awakened by a strange screaming. Pandorica was on top of me straddling me, making strange movements with her hips, and her face looked as if she was in a combination of pain and pleasure. It took me a minute before I realized what she was doing... she was mating with me. During the night she had stripped me naked and somehow found out how to... I almost hate to use the words... make love to me.

"What are you doing?" I asked.

"We mate with Humans to get a hybrid," she said. "We have about a thousand hybrids who live with us." I asked her if the Human females I had met earlier were hybrids. "Yes, they are. They are treated just as if they are full bloods." She was still on top of me grinding slowly and smiling. I just laid back and looked at the ceiling. After all, if Captain Kirk could do it so could I.

It lasted about another hour before I was able to get dressed and walk out into the Zartoon city with Pandorica. It looked as if they had a celebration planned. Pandorica said that it was because we had a successful mating. I wasn't sure how they knew, but they did. "You will mate with many more in the next few days," she said. "It is truly an honor." I figured that I didn't have much of a choice, so I resigned myself to getting laid more than any other man had ever been.

I was really surprised at the way the Zartoon were. They were so much like Humans. I could see examples of love, jealousy, drunkenness, happiness, and even a complex family and social structure. I actually felt that I was back on earth... strange huh... but it was a really good feeling.

Finally, Pandorica came over and led me down a path to a large glass building. "This is where our young are born," she said. I looked in and saw dozens... no... hundreds of eggs scattered across a fur lined floor. She took me by the hand and she pointed to one over in the corner. "That one is ours. It will be a fine young male." It was strange for me, but, for some reason, my chest was full of pride. I leaned over and kissed Pandorica. It was something I don't think she had ever experienced before, because she blushed a darker green and turned shyly away from me.

ENTRY 8
06.03.63.05.13

I have spent the last few days living with, and learning from the Zartoon . They seem to be a peaceful species who live by the Earth saying, "Live and let live." Even when one of them had a problem with another one it was settled by discussion only. Pandorica said that it had been that way for at least ten thousand generations. The way I figured it was that these creatures seemed more advanced than any civilization on Earth.

I was allowed to wander around the city without an escort. I spent the afternoon talking with the hybrids and some of Humans who lived in the Zartoon city. Each and every one of them said the same thing... Zartoon were friendly and caring of the Humans who decided to live amongst them.

"How does the Human population maintain itself," I asked one of the older of the Humans. He just laughed as he replied.

"We do not mate with the Zartoon because we have to," he said. "That is just a benefit. We Humans have our own families and do mate with other Humans. As a matter of fact, we marry in the ancient Yartook traditions. We have been here for less than 500 generations, but we are happy here. We are not treated like the humans in the city say we are. We are not captives. We are not slaves. We choose to live here, and stay separate from the Humans in the Human city. In the last generations the Humans in their city have become monsters. They mistreat the Zartoon who live there and use them as slaves and sexual objects. That was the main reason we left and came here." I graciously thanked the man and went on my way.

The rest of the day and evening I spent with Pandorica talking about her culture, the arts, the poetry. From what I heard and seen the Zartoon in their city were decent "people" who have a heart and soul the same as many Humans I vaguely have flash memories of.

I will tell you meeting those Humans made me wonder what happened to the Earth I loved. Did they finally blow it up... no, I could see it every night... so odds were we had poisoned the planet so badly that we couldn't live there anymore. Is that what happened is that why I am here. But I still look across the galaxy at the blue star before I go to sleep, and I wonder.

I woke up this morning with Pandorica standing beside my bed. She had a young boy standing next to her. "This is your son," she said as she gently pushed him toward my bed. I have to say he was a fine looking boy. He had curly blonde hair and he stood somewhere about four feet tall.

"Fa Nex, he has just been released from the nursery. I grabbed him before any of the others could take him. I cannot be the one who raises him. I just wanted him to see you."

"I am not allowed to bring him here, but I like you Fa Nex and I wanted you to be proud of your son," she said with a smile. "They will drive him out if they find out that you have seen the boy."

"Who?" I asked, as I smiled and looked into the boy's eyes. They were different to mine, but they were still beautiful. He stood strong, and when he turned around I could see the effect of a Human/Zartoon mating. Although he looked Human enough, he had a line of spinal plates running from his neck on down. I don't know why I never said anything to the boy as she dressed him.

"They are the Council Fa Nex," she said, answering my question, she looked nervous as she spoke. "The young are usually raised by special guardians chosen by the Council. It is the law here. I was not chosen so I cannot raise him under Zartoon tradition because he is a hybrid." She smiled nervously once again and then left the room with the boy. After they had gone, I realized I did not even know my son's name.

It took a while for me to totally come to my senses and get dressed. By the time I did, there were two heavily armed Zartoon standing at my door. "You come with us," the bigger one of the two said. When I asked what was going on, he slapped me to the ground and growled at me, while the other was lifting me to my feet. "You come with us now. The Council wants to talk with you." Looking at their faces, I knew better than to argue, so I straightened myself out and went with them. I also had the thought that maybe I had been wrong about the Zartoon being a very advanced species.

The Council was a room filled with Zartoon, Hybrids and Humans. I was shackled before I was allowed to enter then I was dragged in and slammed to the floor before three of who I guess were the leaders. "Fa Nex," one of them started. "There were a dozen Human, Hybrid and Zartoon hatchlings taken from the nursery. Do you know anything about them?"

Pandorica was standing in the back of the room. The boy was gone, but she was standing there.

"I saw the nursery yesterday," I said. "I admired how it worked and then I went back to my room. I never saw the hatchlings or even heard about them."

"Who took you there," he asked. I looked up and right into Pandorica's eyes. They were sad, hurt and pleading so I told the three of them that I was just wandering around and stumbled upon it. I don't think he believed me because he raised his hand as did everyone else on the Council. The guards who had brought me into the room, grabbed me and dragged me out just as hard as they had brought me in.

"Where are you taking me?" I asked as I struggled a bit. "I have the right to know."

Neither of them answered me. They just dragged me and tossed me into a large underground room with no windows and no artificial light. All I know is that I could hear other voices and sense movement. Once I heard the door lock I settled into a corner, tried to get my eyes adjusted to the faint light the rocks gave off and made myself comfortable for the night.

ENTRY 10
15.03.63.18.13


I don't know how long I was locked in that cell. It felt like a week, maybe more, but I tried to keep count from the changes in the guards, so I think it's the 5th.

They have taken me for questioning every day. They always asked me the same questions and I always gave them the same answers. Somehow though I managed to convince them that I was not from Zartoon. I was raised on Yartook and that I had no idea how I got here, but I did find out what happened to the Earth. Yeah, it was still a blue/green ball, but a plague released from some bomb spread across the entire planet and wiped out every form of animal life on the surface.... Humans, animals, insects and even bacteria were eliminated.

As I said before, for some reason, I cannot remember anything more than bits and pieces about my past on Earth. No doubt I had lost loved ones there, but my mind was blank, all I remember is I was Williams from Phoenix. I do not even know my first name. Other than that, just the bits and pieces that suddenly flash into my mind. No doubt not remembering is a blessing. It allowed me to laugh and not cry at the thought that even the mighty cockroach was made extinct. Everybody was wrong... all we needed was a plague to get rid of that damn pest... we just didn't know it.

I was taken from my cell on that last day. It was the middle of the night and the stars were shining bright. Phobos and Deimos were high in the sky. Deimos was in the middle of a lunar eclipse. It was so beautiful. In the distance I could see the glow of the Human city. The funny thing is... I don't have a desire to go there. Even though the Zartoon are suddenly not as I had perceived them at first. Sad really, I had such high hopes that maybe here on Zartoon things would be different.

Pandorica met me about a mile from the jail, for lack of a better word. She told me that there were a few more of the young taken since they took me so that proved that I had nothing to do with it.

Strangely, she looked almost beautiful in the light of the moons. I don't know if it was lunacy or what it was but I walked her down to the banks of one of the waterways and I took her in my arms and kissed her. She was taken aback to say the least.

"We do not just mate where I come from," I said. "It is romantic and, if you do it right, it can be very pleasurable." She told me that she didn't understand so I took her in my arms and kissed her again. Slowly I removed her clothes and I let my hands touch the rest of her body. Yes, it was rather strange touching a non-Human the way I was touching her but somehow it seemed right. I laid her down on the rocks and moved on top if her. It was so easy to mate with her and it was natural and so good. I was nearly in paradise and by the sounds she was making she was too.

That night, under the two moons of Zartoon we cuddled and talked. We made love a few more times before we dozed off to sleep and, believe it or not, we were both happy.

ENTRY 11
16.03.63.04.23

I woke up before Pandorica. There was the sound of some kind of ships flying overhead, and the sounds of gunfire in the distance. It was still dark. The sun was just starting to create an orange glow on the other side of the mountains. The sounds sounded like they were coming from those mountains. I woke up Pandorica. She also heard the noises all she could say was, "Oh no, not again."

She told me that a few times a year the Humans scrimmage near Zartoon cities, show what kind of power they have. It was not meant for anyone to get hurt or killed. It was what females call a bravado contest.

As Pandorica had been speaking, all of a sudden, there was a sound that was louder than any we had heard before and the sky lit up as bright as if the sun was at its highest point.

"Oh no," I said. "Not here! They could not be that fucking stupid... not here!" Pandorica looked at me with a look of pure confusion. "Pandorica, one thing I do remember is that sound,' I told her "Oh yes, how I remember that sound, the asses in control on Earth developed a weapon that could kill millions with a single explosion. It started there during a war and it just grew. No one knew how bad it was until a small country tested one on their soil and the country was burned to ashes in less than 30 seconds. A million people died and those who did live were burnt so badly it was hard to tell that they were Humans."

"This was on Yartook," she asked.

"Yes," I said. "When the last war started all of the countries on Yartook had those weapons and they used them. 90% of the population the planet was killed."

Pandorica had not said anything, she just held my hand tightly and we ran back to the Zartoom city. When we got there we saw that the walls of the city had been burnt... even though the sound and light was maybe a hundred miles away... the city was still affected. The people of the city were just walking around like zombies. It wasn't because of any radiation or anything like that... it was pure and utter shock.

We walked into the Council Chamber and it was empty. The members, from what I was told, were taken underground for their safety. Pandorica and I just stood there holding each other. There was nothing else to do so we just sat down and looked at each other, not knowing how much time was passing, until the moons rose and Zartoon was having its usual beautiful night. Too bad the night didn't realize the terror that the faint light of the sun had brought to this planet and her people.

ENTRY 12
16.03.63.16.23


I spent the afternoon checking the Zartoon and the Humans in the Zartoon city. They were lucky. The blast was not strong enough to do any real damage which was a surprise to me. I figured that there would be some with radiation poisoning, but no one was sick. Still, I had Pandorica get the word out for everyone to make a drink out of charcoal from the many fires around town. I wasn't 100% sure that it would do any good, one of the hybrids had suggested it, and I vaguely remembered having heard it somewhere myself, so maybe, just maybe, there would be some truth in it.

After that I went to a storage area looking for what the Zartoon called a land traveler, I had seen some of the Zartoon using them a couple days before. I didn't know how they worked or what to do to keep them going but I needed transport. There was something I wanted to do... something I needed to do.

Anyway, I went down and "borrowed" one of the travelers. The controls were pretty much like my motorcycle at home. So, I hopped on and drove out of the shop, past the city gates and into the desert. I could feel the cold air against my cheek as I saw the speedometer pass 100 and then 150. I didn't know what the measurements were but I knew that I was flying.

In the distance I could see a plume of solid black smoke that almost blacked out the sun. Thank God that the moons were out because they gave me enough light to travel safely. I adjusted my course to head toward the smoke, and then it was just holding on and letting the machine do the rest.

The trip took about two hours before I got to the site. It was a small town. Going by the size of it, there were maybe five or six hundred who lived there, but now they were just burnt bodies that looked like if you touched them they would crumble into dust. I could see the bodies of Zartoon men, women and children and an equal number of Human and hybrid bodies. The thing that shook me the most were the mothers who were burnt holding their babies in their arms. It was just so sad seeing all of that life destroyed in less than a second.

I couldn't look at the buildings, to tell the sad truth, there was not one building left standing. Actually, they were either melted into slag or blown away in the wind.

I was so devastated by all that I had seen that I was crying when I got back on the traveler, revved up the engines and started back to the city. I had no idea why these people had to die and what hatred caused it, but there was nothing I could do so I gunned the engines and left the town as fast as I could.

My only thought on the way back was that those people were innocent. They didn't look like they were hurting anyone. They were just needless deaths... wasted lives to soothe someone's bigoted hatred and fear.

.

## ENTRY 13
## 17.03.63.07.23


I spent the night out in the desert. It was kind of soothing. The temperature was around 60 degrees and the breezes were slow and gentle. The only sounds I could hear were the travelers from the Zartoon city and some kind of transportation from the Human city, but they were a lot fainter.

I slept well, considering what I had seen the night before. It is extremely hard to get images like that out of your mind once you had seen death like that but, for my own sanity, I had to push those images into my subconscious and get back to surviving myself.

I made it back to the part of the city where Pandorica lived around 11:00 AM and, the minute I parked the traveler, Pandorica came running over to me, throwing her arms around me in a hug but she didn't dare kiss me. Not in the open and surely not in where she would be recognized. She took me by the arm and we went to see the Council. Once there I was asked to give a report of what I had seen.

"There was a settlement," I said. "It isn't there anymore!"

"Was it Human or Zartoon," they asked.

"From what I could see it was a combination of both," I replied. "They seemed to have been family units of both Human and Zartoon, many with young children and some females carrying their young." I told them that everyone was killed and that they all died within seconds. They just sat there silently, just as if they were in shock. Then, one of them started talking.

"In that village were individuals from both our city and the Human city," he said. "Sadly, the Humans in the major Human city near that village keep Zartoon purely for the Humans' pleasure, much as they would animal breeding stock. They are caged and only released to mate and then they are once again locked away. They do the same thing until they cannot mate any longer, and then they are killed. You have seen how we live here Fa Nix, we do not treat Humans that way.

That village was made up of those who were not interested in just mating. The Zartoon and the young defiant Humans they created the village of Elidibsatianouka because they had fallen in love and wanted to be together no matter what. The zealot Humans in their city could not allow this to happen so they must have destroyed the village without any warning."

I saw that that topic was upsetting to the Council, yet even so, they still wanted to know more. So I explained to them that I had looked and could not find a weapon, but I could guess what it was. I looked into the mourning faces of the Council. I told them of the hydrogen bombs of the mid-1940's and how it destroyed entire cities without even hitting the ground.

"Can you make us one of those weapons," one of them asked.

Now, for some reason I knew the basics of what to do. I do not understand why, but I did, maybe I had seen things on TV or in the movies, or maybe I was in a war, but for some reason, I knew how to make a very primitive bomb. All I knew was that I didn't want to give him that knowledge. I recall what it did to Earth when the people were always fighting and deathly afraid of other countries, and through terrorism, there were so many deaths that it finally grew so bad that a full planet nuclear winter was eventually inevitable. Maybe that is just what happened to the Earth I thought, as I replied to his question.

"No, sir, normal people like me were not allowed to know how to make such a terrible device, and we were killed if we did have that knowledge."

I don't know if he believed me or not, but he looked at me and waved his hand. I was escorted out and led to Pandorica, who was waiting outside.

We spent the rest of the day together as she taught me some of Zartoon history. According to their history, Zartoon was a vast and very successful empire before the Humans arrived. I asked her how long the Zartoon had been on the planet. She laughed and replied that the Zartoon people had lived on the planet for over 200,000 generations. Then I asked her how long the Humans had been there. "500 generations," she said. Her eyes lowered and it was easy to see that she was feeling strong emotions toward what had happened earlier.

I didn't ask her any more questions. We sat and talked about happier things. I recited poetry to her and she sang strange sounding Zartoon opera to me. Her voice was so lyrical, usually I don't like opera, but when she sang it was really beautiful!

## ENTRY 14
18.03.63.15.58


I managed to get to sleep and, for the first time, it was a peaceful rest. I guess it was Pandorica's soft voice that helped erase the memories of everything I had seen. The only problem was that I was awakened by a gentle shaking about an hour ago. My eyes opened and I thought that it was Pandorica, but instead I saw the face of Fraderk the leader of the Council.

"Fa Nex," he said. "Come with me. I have something we must talk over."

"Yes, sir," I said. My eyes were still foggy as I stood and walked into the courtyard with him. "How may I help you?"

"There is a legend here," it said as he looked at Phobos and Deimos as they were just breaking the horizon. "It was written that a time would come when the twins would come together and, at that time a warrior would come to our people who would stop the suffering that so many have endured. As I said, that moment would be when the twins come together, but also when a light would appear in the west. I pronounce that the light appeared last night and..." He looked once again at the moons. "... the twins will be as one within the next three nights. Fa Nex, I know that you are the warrior who was proclaimed so many generations ago."

I denied that I was then, or ever had been a

warrior. "Fraderk, I have never touched another Human to harm him," I said.

"We do not need you to fight for us," he said. "There are those who would do that in your place. All we need is for you to awaken the gods and they will protect us."

"And just how do I do that," I asked, half for real and the other half sarcastically,

"There is a relic from the days just after our people came to Zartoon," Fraderk said. "It is buried in a cave about six days travel from here in the directions of the setting sun."

I had to ask - what was this artifact, and what did it mean, before they came to Zartoon?

"It is said," he had stated, "that it is a sword made from the horn of a pure white horned reptile. Our ancestors created it while they lived on Yartook." I looked confused; as Fraderk went on to explain. "We were a smaller branch of the reptiles who ruled the world at the time. The time came when Yartook was changing, so we were forced to leave. Once we arrived here, we saw a shimmering in the air near where we now have our settlements; this shimmering was understood to a blessing from our gods. One of our ships landed, followed by many more until our gods granted us this world to have as our own. We have been here ever since."

We talked another 20 minutes or so before I graciously found a way to go back to my room and try to finish my night's sleep. Pandorica was waiting on our bed, and she smiled and gently caressed my body, it took a while, but sleep finally did find me, and that pleased this so called newly found warrior sent to awaken the Gods.

## ENTRY 15
## 20.03.63.15.58

It has already been two days since I left the Zartoon city on my quest to find the white sword. So far it had been a smooth trip on the traveler. That was until earlier this afternoon. The thing was, I knew it had to happen and it did. I ran into a patrol of Humans who were armed beyond anything I could have ever imagined.

I was traveling at a pretty good clip when they let loose with an electromagnetic pulse. The second it hit me, my traveler stopped dead, throwing me into the sand. Immediately, I had two of the patrol standing on either side of me with guns drawn with their barrels pressing into my neck.

"Remove your helmet," one of them commanded. I was quick to obey and when I did the two men stepped back in shock. "You... you're a... Human," one of them said as shock rolled all over him. "Where did you come from? How did you get that outfit and that machine," he asked.

I had to think quick to keep from getting shot. I tried thinking up lies, but none would work in my mind so I was damn sure they wouldn't fool these two geniuses so I decided to tell the truth. "Where am I from," I asked back to him. "Well, I'm from Elkston, Maine."

The soldier asked me, "By the one true God, where is that"

Thinking I could have some fun, I decided to be a bit of a prankster. So I answered that it really wasn't far from the Canadian border. He didn't seem to know what the Canadian border was, so I said that it was between the St. Lawrence Seaway and the Atlantic Ocean. That got him really confused and also very angry, so a metal plated glove across my face proved to be the only sensible answer. Of course it knocked me out cold, and I guess that is how I ended up naked on a white marble floor with a couple of hundred people staring at me.

ENTRY16
24.03.63.15.58

I have been here for four days now. I have been poked, prodded, questioned and tortured. The worst of the torture was being paraded through the street, naked and with a collar around my neck. I was placed in with a group of Zartoon and some other Humans. We were spat at, hit, and were pelted with rocks as we walked. A few younger Humans ran out and struck with sticks in the legs and groins. Then they would run back to their parents and stand there laughing. There was no way that this was the behavior of Humans I remembered back on Earth... at least I thought that until flashbacks came of our history. The Civil War, Nazis, The Atomic Bomb, Mass murders in the Soviet Union, Poland's Ethnic cleansing, Pol Pot, and barbarians like Attila The Hun.

Now in my Zartoon Human prison, the most painful torture was my solitude. There was not one time that anyone spoke to me or even looked at me. It was as if I was a non-person. I could hear the Zartoon prisoners or maybe they were slaves talking to each other and I could hear the guards and the people walking by. They spoke a kind of diluted American language, but it was enough for me to understand, but they treated me like nothing more than an inarticulate animal who wasn't worth their time.

When I was allowed out to stretch, outside, through the rock wall I could see one of the streets. There were many Humans walking around. Not all of them, but a large number of them had Zartoon on leashes following close behind them as if they were puppies.

I was in a lot of pain, due to the beatings I had received. It felt like my skin and muscles were on fire, but I lived through it. On the night of my fourth day I was dragged to the city gates, beaten viciously once again and left for dead. Fortunately, they did leave my clothes and this notepad, which was still in my back trouser pocket, luckily I have it and can record all I went through while a prisoner of the Humans living in their Human Zartoon City. The one thing they didn't give me was my traveler, so I now I have to walk to finish my quest.

Before I left that diabolical city, I spread my arms as if I was on a cross, drew in as much air as I could and screamed, "Where did all of the Humanity go?" I didn't get an answer but I did get a pot of water poured on me. After all I had experienced, how could have I ever expected any better?

I started out once again to the south. As I walked, I could hear darts being fired from the city wall. A few of them did hit me in the back and on my legs. It was painful, but I just ignored them until I was out of their range, then I sat down and gently pulled all of them out one by one. I know they had throw me away to die, But

I was the Zartoon's warrior, and after my fellow Humans' treatment of me, nothing was going to stop me helping the Zartoon, after all I was the "Chosen one".

My journey that day was a little over twenty miles, and when I finally decided to sleep it was on a pile of small rocks. Hell, that was the only ground around that wasn't a marsh of some kind. So, I drank from the marsh. The water was bitter, but it was what I needed so I drank it, and I ate some weeds that grew along its banks. So, after I ate and drank, I looked at the stars, gazed down on blue star Yartook with a desire to be there once more, despite what might have happened there, and finally fell asleep.

ENTRY 17
28.03.63.18.31


I am so hungry. It has been a couple days since I got out of jail. Yeah, they gave me some food and water, but it wasn't near enough to survive on and that ran out late yesterday afternoon. Hell, I can't even be sure what the time or date really is. Unfortunately, they took my watch and never returned it.

Let's see Earth was 24 hours a day, 365 days a year. If I remember right the days are just about the same length of time as on earth, so the calendar should be pretty much be the same but, how long is the their year? I remember that an old teacher of mine said that a year on Mars was almost two years on earth. Now, Pandorica has assured me, so many times that this is not Mars, this is Zartoon! Well, whatever the hell it is, I just wish my watch was still on my wrist. I suppose from now on I will just have to stop thinking in Earth time and start adjusting to the fact that the Zartoon and even the Humans do not seem to make a major deal of time.

Anyway, screw all of that. I have to find some food soon or I may have to go back to the Humans just to stay alive. Which would not be good, as now I have a mission, as the supposedly Zartoon savior's something I have to do. Maybe it will prove them right and actually save some lives, maybe not, but I won't know until

I get back to the Zartoon city with my mission accomplished.

I resorted to flipping over rocks to try and find some traces of moss. There was some, thank God, so I was able to get some moisture from the roots of the moss.

I have changed my travel times. I walk at night and sleep during the day. It was bitter cold as I walked, but it was better than roasting under the sun... especially around midday. It wasn't the heat. It was more that I was getting severe sunburns.

When I started out that last night I saw the edge of a forest on the horizon. I tried to remember where I was. Was there a canal there just beyond my line of sight? It couldn't have been that far away. I walked maybe four hours to get there, but it was a forest and it was lush with ferns, trees and grasses. The air was full of animal noises and I even saw a couple monkey-like creatures swinging in the trees. And there was water. Such sweet smelling water I dropped to my knees and drank my fill as soon as I saw it.

I heard voices from the other side of the lake. I couldn't figure out if they were Human or Zartoon but they were voices, and I knew that I had to be careful until I found out who they were? But right now, all that will wait until tomorrow.

## ENTRY 18
29.03.63.05.45


Oh my God. Whoever they are, these human or Zartoon they were up all night celebrating. I am not sure what? But whatever it was they were happy, they are quiet now so I am going to go over and take a look.

Later: They weren't too far away. Just over a small hill. I am surprised that I didn't see the glow of a fire or anything like that. It only took a couple of minutes for me to reach the top of the hill, once there I found a nice big rock to hide behind. I was so close that, even if I had brought them, I didn't need binoculars or anything like that. What I could see was some kind of still, and I sure could smell the sweet perfume of a good old fashioned bourbon.

There were bodies laying all over the clearing. They weren't dead or anything like that. They were just in a nice deep sleep. I heard noises coming up over the hill as they were moaning, stirring and snoring in their sleep.

They were young. Maybe only 17 or 18 years old and they were a mixture of both Humans and Zartoon, male and female and they were all exceedingly drunk.

I tried my best to be quiet as I walked through the site. A few of them stirred just a bit, but fell back to sleep before they had the chance to see me. Outside of the clearing I saw a couple dozen travelers and some things that looked like horses except they had blue coats of hair with violet mane and tail. To tell the truth, they were very impressive except for one thing.... They had very big mouths.

As if in unison they raised up on the rear legs and screamed at the sky. This woke up everyone in the clearing. Even though they were suffering from hangovers (who would have guessed that Zartoon, just like Humans, could have a hangover) as I was walking amongst them, I was visible, so some staggered up to see who I was and what I was doing. That was fine with me. I was curious about them too!

Now, they were not at all aggressive. They were actually very passive, kind of like the hippies of the late 1960's. Confusing as it was once again here were Humans and the Zartoon living together in total harmony so different to what I had experienced when I was held captive by the city Humans with their enslaved Zartoon.

They circled around me, when they realized I was not a threat, we sat down on the ground and started talking. It was an interesting chat. One of the Human youths had found an old copy of a movie called "Woodstock." They decided that they liked the idea and created a society based on what they had seen. They even found a way to duplicate the dress and the music of the time.

I spent the entire day with them. Telling them as much as I could remember about my

49

life as a hippie back in those wild and crazy days they asked a lot of questions some, of course I could not answer, as I did not really remember people close to me at the time, only the fond memories of the period and my drug induced flower power and the exhilaration of feeling free, for the first time free from rules and hypocrisy... I answering their questions as best I could and believe me... there were a lot of questions.

We ate, drank and partied all day. They were really good people and it was nice to see the peace and love of the 1960's alive again. At the end of the day we all lay down together in a circle round the fire to keep warm, and I fell asleep wishing that I wouldn't have to leave, but knowing that I did.

ENTRY 19
30.03.63.00.10

The next morning, when I awoke, I decided it was time to continue my journey in search of the white sword. The Zartoon and the Humans were very kind and gave me two days' worth of food, that weird horse thing, and a ten gallon container of water. They also offered me some of the herbs that they were smoking and, of course, I accepted. I was still tired, but I wasn't stupid!

The entire group surrounded me when I was starting to leave and they were chanting something that sounded really strange yet was very relaxing.

"You are one of us," one of them said. You will be welcomed back any time you wish to return."

Hell, that was the only welcoming thing I had encountered, other than Pandorica, since I got to this God forsaken planet. I told them that I would be honored to come back and see them after my mission was over. One of the Zartoon females and a Human female ran over to me and kissed my cheek, and then I was off again.

I got my bearings at last, which had been almost impossible to do as the terrain was new to me, and I started traveling in as good of a straight line as I could. It was still a two day trip, I guessed from what I had been told, and

I wanted to get it over with as soon as possible.

The entire day I thought back to those people and the stories they told me, but the one that interested me the most was the one about the white sword. They told me that it was in an ancient castle and was protected by a kind of spectre, who refused to let anyone ever even see the sword.

"We just went to see it, to worship it as it should be, and they attacked us," one of them said. "They didn't harm our bodies. They were more insidious. They attacked our minds. They made us doubt and fear each other. They made us see creatures that weren't there. They even made us see our friends die when they were still alive. You cannot protect yourself from them."

Now, this made me nervous as I was traveling closer and closer to that castle, but I knew what I was there for, and I was going to get that white sword no matter what evil might befall me.

The food they gave me was good, but the water was sooooo much better. I had to ration it, but God, that was so hard to do.

The ground I was traveling on was even worse, I'm sure, than our Death Valley back home. There was nothing, nothing at all. No grass, no animals, no water... nothing, but I found a rock which had some shade so I camped down there for the night.

The sky was the darkest black I had ever seen. I could even see Yartook clearly as it shone, just a small blue glow in the distant universe. Still, all I could think of was Pandorica and how much I missed her, but even those thoughts disappeared when I rolled a smoke and lit it up. Before long I was not asleep, but I was relaxed... something my body truly needed so I just settled back, finished my smoke and turned off the rest of the night.

ENTRY 20
31.03.63.19.10

Man, what a hangover! I think maybe I smoked a couple too many of those things they gave me. Yeah, it was fun, but now... holy crap!

Well, I got myself straightened out, fed whatever it was, and started out to the south. It wasn't long until I saw one minaret, then another and another. They glistened like gemstones against the red sky. They were still miles and miles away, but they were beautiful!

I crossed over a ridge and found myself standing at the edge of a mile-wide canal. I think part of my memory is coming back, but no personal stuff. I wonder why? Oh well, maybe in time. Schiaparelli was right. There was a canal on Mars! I had no idea who built it or when it was built, but it was there and, from what I could see, it was heading straight south.

In the "water" of the canal I could see iridescent blue/green creatures. They looked beautiful. They looked sort of human, but in place of arms were gentle, veil-like fins and each had a tail with flukes that looked as if they were powerful and still very fragile. Each one looked at me as it passed. They all smiled, with their faces just below the surface. At that moment I truly could understand where the legend of mermaids came from.

I rode my animal alongside the canal for

miles. I saw so many different kinds of life along the way. There were even a couple of birdlike creatures that buzzed my head as I rode by. The funny thing was… no matter what I saw I never had a shred of fear. I felt completely relaxed.

I am probably still a day and a half away from the castle and it is so massive that I could easily see what I guessed was the top half of the building. I did see one thing that confused me… every hour a ball of plasma shot from one of the minarets and out into space where it exploded into a fantastic light show. Even in the middle of the day it was easy to see and it easily took my breath away.

*How could these creatures be anything other than friendly,* I thought. *Nothing could create beauty like that and have hatred in their hearts?*

There was plenty to eat for both me and the creature, the grass was as soft as the best down mattress I could remember and damn, it was just so damn restful. "Why don't I crash here," I asked. I think the creature must have understood the question because it walked over to a nearby tree, walked around it a couple of times and then just dropped to the ground and went to sleep. I took his cue and did the same thing. God, it was so nice for a change!

ENTRY 21
01.04.63.18.52

That was one hell of a sleep. I could hear thunder in the distance and believe it or not I was still feeling completely relaxed.

The towers were now crystal clear. They looked like I could reach out and touch them, but I knew I had another few hours to go. I spent the morning relaxing and eating, before getting back on my ride and starting off.

The day was cool, especially for being in the middle of the desert. I once again saw several "birds" flying overhead. I swear that at least a dozen of them were as big as the old jets they had on Earth. They didn't seem interested in me in the least. It almost looked as if they were all migrating toward the castle. I don't understand why, but that was where they were headed.

It took me just about six hours to make it to the front of the main gate, which was made of a light blue crystal, or rather, hundreds of light blue crystals.

I left my ride, tying its harness to a small log beside the gate. The gate looked massive but it swung easily and didn't seem to have any weight on it at all. When I walked in, my mouth dropped in awe. The entire inside of the castle was lined with the same crystals as the gate, and hanging from the ceiling was a magnificent white dragon. Its size was beyond anything anyone could ever imagine and it was surrounded by smaller dragons.

While I stood there and looked around, taking in everything that I could, a young woman walked in behind me. She had jet black hair and eyes, but her skin was the color of the finest ivory. "Who are you and what are you doing here," she asked. Her voice was sweet, yet had a kind of strength to it that no Earth woman ever had.

"My name is Williams and I was sent here on a quest to retrieve a white sword," I said.

The minute I finished the answer, the woman was surrounded by hundreds of spirits. "The white sword is not allowed to be touched," she said in a much firmer, less sweet voice. "You must leave now before you will be killed." I kind of believed that she meant what she said, then she continued. "This has been the law for millions of trips around the sun." The thing was, she wasn't really looking at me. I swear that she was looking through me.

"May I ask your name," I asked.

She looked straight at me. "There have been many before you and many have died trying to steal the sword."

"That's nice to know," I said with a laugh. I had suddenly figured out that she wasn't "real". She was some kind of hologram, but I was sure that the spirits were real. I didn't think much; I just opened the gate again and went outside. Setting up camp was easy, my sleeping bag and lantern and I was settled in for the night.

I would gain all my strength back after my journey. Then, with a clear head in the morning I would figure out what to do to retrieve the white sword, and once it was in my possession, help save the people of Zartoon.

ENTRY 22
02.04.63.12.45

Unfortunately I just could not sleep at all last night. So after an hour or so, I just sat on a rock near the entrance and watched the people entering and exiting the building. One thing I noticed was that they were all dressed exactly the same... light gray robe, a hood and sandals. I couldn't see their face so I couldn't tell if they were Zartoon or Human or even if they were male or female. They all looked that much alike.

I waited until just before sunrise, just observing everything that was happening. Luckily, one of the beings suddenly started walking towards me. It was alone, so when it got close enough, I jumped across, attacked the creature and stole its robe.

The robe had been easy to get off, and when I did I saw that the "creature" was a young adult Human female. Now, I did not hurt her... I just knocked her hard enough to make her unconscious so that I could tie her up and gag her. After all, I didn't want her yelling for help.

I then decided to walk around the towers as I didn't want to reveal where I had set up camp. It took me about an hour, but luckily I was wearing the robe, so once I got to the gate it was easy to take the posture of the others and simply walk in.

That hologram was still there, but this time

she seemed to be preaching to all the people who walked in. It was a message of peace and love that reminded me of the crap I heard in Sunday school. I couldn't take it then and I sure as hell couldn't stand it now.

Like I said, I was doing the exact same as the others in the room which meant that I had to keep my eyes facing the ground but I could still see a lot. I saw her figure on the floor as well as those of the spirits that were still flying around her.

Finally, after an hour she stopped preaching and told her followers to split into groups. As she said that each of the people dropped their robes. There were an equal number of men and women in the group. Of course I had to disrobe also. I was nervous about it, but once I did neither she nor the spirits seemed to notice me so I quietly joined one of the groups and continued to listen to her diatribe.

"The Human race needs you," she said. "There are no more people on Earth to colonize here. I need you all to go as groups. It is your responsibility to create life and help the Human race thrive on this barren world. Now go and do what I ask."

Now, it didn't sound quite like she was asking me. It sounded like a command that all of those around her were more than willing to obey. It was almost like watching robots the way they listened with wide opened eyes and a complete lack of any intelligence.

Anyway, I followed the group, but I didn't go into the room. Once I was out of sight of that main chamber I took off on my own.

It is now 12.40. So I am going to end this for now. I will report more later.

## ENTRY 23
02.04.63.06.23

So far I have been pretty much been able to wander around here as I wanted. I saw a few of those spirits floating around, but they just ignored me. This place is a lot bigger than I first thought it was. There are miles and miles of hallways and innumerable doors. Most of them are locked, and the ones that are unlocked are pretty much nothing. They appear to be living quarters, yet other than the people who come in through the front door, I have not seen a living being anywhere. This place keeps getting stranger and stranger!

Finally, I found a door at the far end of one of the hallways. There were two spirits standing on either side of the door and each was holding a sword in front of it. They kind of reminded me of those tombs in France, where the Knights Templar are buried, except the swords I was looking at seemed a lot more menacing and a whole lot more deadly.

Lowering my head, I walked toward the door. When I was about twenty feet away the guards noticed me and raised their swords. "Stop your approach," they both said at the same time. I slowed down, but I still kept walking. "Stop your approach," they said again. The thing was the tone of their voices never changed. A couple of more steps and they repeated their command, still in the same voice as before. I was about two feet away from them when they moved again, shoving their swords into my abdomen. I bent over in expected pain fortunately there was no pain and no blood. As I raised myself back up, they thrust again and again, still with no results.

"What in the hell," I yelled. I stood there for a minute watching their swords enter and then exit my body. Then I realized "These bastards are just holograms. They can't hurt me."

Once again, I heard "Stop your approach." Again, I didn't listen and, as I reached for the doorknob a sudden rush of courage came over me.

"Fuck you both," I said loudly. The doorknob opened easily and, once the door was open, I saw why there were guards protecting the room. It was huge… as big as a football field and as high as a five story building. Inside was a massive computer. It was bigger than anything I had ever seen or ever even imagined. My thoughts were childish the moment I saw it. I instantly thought how great any game would be if I was able to play them on this computer. I know it was silly, but hey, I felt relaxed for the first time all day.

It took me a while, but I found the control console. It was covered with several inches of dust. It was obvious no one had been in this room in hundreds of years. It was amazing. That computer had been running and maintaining itself, for all that time.

I am going to have to take my time figuring this thing out so I cannot write anymore. I will make another entry before the moons set in the morning.

It did take me a while, but I finally figured it out. The computer was the control panel for everything in the palace, maybe even the palace itself. I tried a couple of the buttons and, when I pushed them, two guards appeared behind me. They didn't do or say anything... they just stood there so I thought I'd try something. "Go stand guard outside the door," I said. As soon as the last sound came from my lips, they both turned and walked out of the door and took their places on either side. "Do not let anyone in," I ordered. They bowed and then returned to their positions as the door closed behind them.

Then I got a surprise... more of a shock than a surprise. I turned back to the console and there was a figure sitting in the seat. I could see that it was wearing the same type of cloak that I wore when I snuck in. Its back was to me and it seemed to be ignoring me. Slowly I walked up behind the chair and spun it around as quickly as I could. It was a Zartoon. "How did you get in here," I asked.

The figure stood and faced me eye to eye, but I still couldn't see its face. "Fa Nex," it said. "I am here to help you." I grabbed the cloak and threw the hood back. It was Pandorica. I wasn't sure how she got here or what she was doing here. I did know  I was so glad to see a loving, friendly face, especially my Pandorica's.

"Have you found the sword yet?" she asked

I reached over and took her by the hand. "I haven't found it yet," I said with a slight smile. "I was hoping that I could find the answer in here."

"Did you have any luck?" she asked as she gently pulled her hand away.

I questioned myself. *Why would she not want to hold hands with me*, I thought so I just kept looking at her eyes. They were not the same warm eyes, I remembered. Oh yeah, they were still as beautiful, but there was just something strange about them.

"No," I said. "I was still trying to figure the computer out when you showed up. By the way... how did you get in here?"

"Fa Nax, never mind that," she said. "Fa Nax, please you must not activate the full power of the computer. If you do, you will destroy the planet." I was able to think a minute while she continued. "When they created this place they made it a place of peace that could never be destroyed. They made sure that nothing would ever happen to it."

"So they built it to blow up," I asked.

"They built it so that it can defend itself and not be used by those who would disrupt the peace," she said with an intensity that bordered on a manic anger. "You must leave this place." Oh no, This was not the Pandorica I knew back in the city. She was different... totally different.

As she spoke I reached for a big button which was situated next to one of the power level controls. "Fa Nex," she yelled. "You have no idea what you are doing."

I did not give her a chance to say anything else. I put my hand on the button and pushed hard. As soon as I did she just disappeared into empty air. It was then I figured out what she was. The computer had read my mind and brought me someone I would trust. She was just a hologram and I nearly fell for it. A moment later the entire building shook as if it were in a level 5 earthquake. I watched as the walls surrounding me disappeared, followed by the floor, the computer, and everything else. It was as if they were never there, within ten minutes the entire building was gone. All that remained were myself, and outside the hundreds of people who were there to worship.

I was confused, as no doubt so were all the others who had been listening to the hologram preaching. As I looked around this now desolate place, I found a cave which must have been beneath the building the whole time. At that moment the moons were rising, so I decided not to investigate any further that night. Instead, now I am going to get some sleep, as no doubt the cave will still be there in the morning.

## ENTRY 25
03.04.63.22.32

The sun was shining when I woke up. There were still people wandering around, I guess they were trying to figure out where to go or what to do. After all, how could anyone watch their god be erased right in front of them and be of a sound mind... at least for a while? I just sat there watching those poor souls, I know that it really must have hurt them, but in the long run, they will be better off.

The cave was still there, but then again... where would it go? I mean after all it was a cave. Anyway, once I looked closely at it the more there was something strange about it. There were no jagged rocks at the entrance. Hell, there were no rocks at all. There was a small stream that ran into the opening but there were no signs of erosion. It kind of reminded me of spilling a drink in the middle of a parking lot. It just followed a small crack in the soil.

I left my supplies, except for some food, sitting there on the sand. I wasn't afraid that any of those people would steal anything. They had too many other problems to worry about than my meager belongings.

The entrance to the cave was massive. It was a lot bigger than it looked the day before. The rock was dark black with veins of blue spread throughout the surface. I saw a streak of metal, it was silver in color with stains of rust beneath it. That has got to be iron, I thought, yeah, it had to be, that would have been what gave the soil its red color.

The darkness inside started almost immediately, there were cracks every few yards so there was a glimmer of light, still it took a while for my eyes to adjust but when they did and I could see everything. It was dark, but at least I didn't need a torch.

The walls were smooth... too smooth! This cave was not natural, it was made by someone, I am not saying Human or Zartoon, but someone or something made it sometime in the past.

It was kind of hard walking down into the cave. The floor was slick from use, at least I think it was from wear, there were cracks and pits that I had to watch out for. I wasn't sure if they were deep, or if they were just a couple of inches, so I went along carefully making sure that I always had good footing before I took another step.

The funny thing was the path was not going down deeper into the ground. After the first twenty feet or so it leveled off and just went on straight.

I probably walked a couple miles before the cave narrowed, and I ended up on my knees to just make it through. That went on for about five hundred feet before it opened into a gigantic cavern. One could have built a stadium on it, and still have room to spare, it was dim, but there was some light coming through a medium sized crack in the ceiling.

My eyes had to adjust again, but it was a lot faster this time. I could see, there was something at the far side of the cavern. I could just make it out, it looked like a building... kind of a church that had been abandoned centuries before, but as my eyes grew even more accustomed to the light I could see more and more. There were buildings all throughout the cavern. There were houses, shops and only God knows what else, I had stumbled upon an entire underground city.

The first building I approached was a house. There were bodies inside. They were long dead, but perfectly preserved.

I walked in, sat down and talked to some of them, of course they didn't answer, but it made me feel better. Anyway, I had some food and relaxed in a chair next to an open window. Unfortunately, it had been a long day so I started relaxing too much. I knew that I had better write this before I fall asleep.

ENTRY 26
04.04.63.15.15


It was hard to tell if I woke up in the daytime or in the middle of the night, so I am just guessing what time it is that I am writing this.

I am amazed how my eyes have adjusted to the low light. It is just like I am walking around outside just after sunset, but then again, with two moons, the night here is almost like daytime, especially when the moons are full.

The steps of the temple were cold... very cold. I couldn't tell what they were made of but I assume it was a kind of granite because of how smooth they were. Anyway, I woke up, got a little something to eat and started looking around the temple.

It was amazingly beautiful. There were statutes along either side of the halls. In fact, there were hundreds of them. Some were made of stone and others were made of metal. I swear I also saw one or two that I think were made of gold, but I couldn't be sure.

At last I made it to the altar chamber. Inside was a large statue. It was nearly as tall as the room was wide and beneath it was a sentence carved into the rock. It said Tywyllwch -- bydded i dduw tangnefedd. I had no idea what that meant, but by the peaceful, loving, happy look on the statue's face I have a feeling that I was looking into the face of an ancient Zartoon god... Maybe the same God we had on Earth, but then again, maybe not.

I was really not sure what to do. The room was so full of artifacts. The sword could have been one of them, but it would take hours, maybe days or more to check everything out. There was one thing I found right next to "God's" left foot. It was a crystal that measured about two feet long. From what I could tell it was as clear as a piece of glass and there were no defects anywhere to be seen. I don't know why, but as soon as I touched it a white glow started appearing in the center and, within minutes there was enough light to see all through the room as well as enough to light the many tunnels leading from it.

I spent the next few hours wandering the hallways. There were so many rooms and so much to see. I could not believe that such a culture could exist anywhere but Earth. Maybe our culture and everything we know... or knew... came from here and we were just transplanted from here? That would be something! I will have to find a nice, comfortable corner, check out what I had found and think about everything before I take another step. I think I will do that and write more here later today.

# ENTRY 27
## 04.04.63.18.15

This entry is going to be short. I searched the room for a couple of hours until I found one thing. I leaned against the base of the statue and it slid back... not far but it moved. I backed away and looked. There was a space beneath the statue and there was a glow coming from beneath it. I pushed the base again and it slid back even more, revealing a stairway that led down into a lower chamber. I have no idea where it led or what was down there, but you know Humans... we are a curious species. I have to go down and see what is there.

I do remember that I am under a time crunch. I have to get back to the Zartoon city, but I still have not found the sword so maybe those stairs would lead me to it.

My recorder I will leave at the entry to the steps, I don't want to risk having it damaged. So I will make another entry when, if, I come back.

I was down there for nine hours, it was beautiful, especially considering it was just a tunnel and a room at the end. All along the route there were paintings, they looked to me like a mixture of prehistoric cave paintings and hieroglyphics. I couldn't read them, but I got the idea that they were talking about a major battle, because they pictured soldiers and bodies with spears and arrows as weapons… except for one. He had no shield and only a white sword for a weapon, I am sure that was the weapon I am looking for.

I am going to have to go back down again, honestly, I could not believe what I saw down there. There were so many swords, armor and so much more. I am going to have to go through every item until I find the white sword.

I was just standing there when I heard a voice and saw a bright light. It was coming from the tunnel. "You must prove that you are a worthy young warrior," it said. "Only the noblest heart will be allowed to take the sacred white sword from its resting place."

"Oh my God," I said to myself. "What on earth do I have to do now?" Then the voice continued.

"The Statue of Marza will judge you as you approach it," it said. "If you are not pure of heart you will not pass with the sword, and you will be trapped in the room at the end of the tunnel forever."

Right then I had second thoughts about going back down there, but I knew that the Zartoon needed that sword, and I had sworn to them that I was going to get it. Then I heard another voice from behind me. I turned and saw Pandorica standing ten feet away. I looked at her and asked, looking straight into her eyes. "Are you my Pandorica or just another hologram?"

"No, no, Fa Nex, I am not a hologram." she answered. "I was worried about you, so I followed you here. I have been at that camp for the last few days... the one with the friendly people. They treated me well and told me where you went. Fa Nex I have come here to be with you, to help you find the sword."

I still wasn't sure if she was real or not, so I walked over and pinched her gently on the ass. It felt as I remembered it did, and she screamed and then laughed, so I knew this was my Pandorica and that she was well and truly real. I was so happy to see her.

I told her that I had found where the sword was, but I would have to rest before I recovered it, so she and I found a nice flat rock and settled down for the rest of the night. A special night of holding her tightly in my arms, a togetherness that I had missed more than I realized.

ENTRY 29
05.04.63.18.25


I cannot believe that Pandorica is here. It was so nice to have held her in my arms last night. You know, I never thought that interspecies love was possible, but I swear that I have fallen in love with her.

We went down into the tunnel today. That room was amazing. We searched through so many things. You could see the history of ancient Zartoon all in that room. There were artifacts, both Human and Zartoon, going back millions of years. Their technology was so far ahead of what we have now, it is hard to believe, but it did prove one thing... at one point Humans and the Zartoon lived together peacefully. Maybe there was a war or something that made Humans flee this planet for millions of years and when they came back... the humans, knew no better than to once again fight the same type wars we had on Earth in the 20th Century.

Suddenly, Pandorica yelled out. "Fa Nex, I've found it, the white sword... it is here," she cried out as she pointed to a glass case in the corner of the chamber. "Oh Fa Nex, I found it!" Her excitement was so contagious that I raced over to her and took her in my arms and kissed her. "Thank you, " I whispered as we both stared across at the magnificent sword.

I went over to the case. The glass was thick

and I couldn't break it so I backed off to try and figure out what to do. Pandorica walked over to the case and placed her hand on the glass. She closed her eyes and whispered something that I couldn't quite hear. As she did what she was doing, the glass just dissolved in front of her. It was then that I realized, that she was the pure soul that had to be the one to get the sword. "I am not going to touch it," I said. "You take it. Pandorica, you are the chosen one."

She reached in and touched the sword. It shimmered with the strangest light I have ever seen. She wrapped her fingers around it. It looked so natural in her hand. The sword came out of the case easily and she, of course, swung the sword as if she was at war.

At the end of the room, by the tunnel, the statue awoke. Its eyes glowed a bright green and its mouth started moving. "You, Zartoon, come before me and bring the sword," it said. Pandorica obeyed. "Are you pure of heart and soul?"

"I am," Pandorica said as she knelt before the statue.

"Come and touch me," the statue said. She did as she was told, and as she did the statue closed its eyes and took a deep breath. "I see that you have made mistakes in your life, but essentially your soul is clean. Do you regret the mistakes you have made?"

Pandorica thought for a moment, and looked at me. Then she turned back to the statue. "I regret all, but the one, that others may consider a mistake ," she said.

"I understand," the statue said, "My child, love is never a mistake," and although Pandorica had never said the word love, the statue must have read her heart and understood what she was feeling, for the statue, then said "I bless you and the love that you have for the Yartook... you both may pass."

ENTRY 30
07.04.63.06.32

Pandorica and I woke up just as the sun was coming up. The light was brighter than usual and there were only a few clouds out on the horizon. The good thing was we had the sword and could finally start back to the Zartoon city.

There were still a lot of the worshipers wandering around outside, in a dazed state, without focus. Suddenly they recognized me and also Pandorica, and a couple of them came running over. "You are the one who destroyed our temple," one of them yelled. I didn't know how to answer so I just looked at the man. "Are you the chosen one," he asked. "I saw you... you are the one who destroyed our temple. I know you are!" Finally, I told him that I indeed was the one who destroyed their temple. He turned to the crowd and yelled. "Jeca ta Hetrea ja loren."

As soon as he yelled that, every one of the worshipers turned and ran toward me. I immediately pulled the sword out and pointed it at them, as I commanded Pandorica to run back into the cave and I would protect her. She did as I said and was well hidden when they reached me, but instead of showing anger they were smiling. "What in the hell?" I asked myself. Then they did the strangest thing...each and every one of them dropped to the ground and started bowing to me.

"Hetrea ja," they all started chanting.

I was just standing there looking at them when Pandorica came back out and stood beside me. "Fa Nex," she said. "They think that you are a god. Only a god could have done what you did. Hetrea ja means almighty God."

"But… I am not a god, and do not want to be " I whispered to Pandorica. "Can you tell them that for me?" She tried, but every time she tried to open her mouth the people started chanting even louder and someone started a new chant calling her Hetera ja's wife.

"If we hint that we are not gods…," Pandorica said. "… I think that they will turn violent and we do not want that."

One of the men who originally walked up to me, came up us and told us that an impromptu celebration was being set up by some of the worshipers to welcome the new gods to their land.

"We can't," I had said. "We have to get home."

"You must," he said as he took both Pandorica and I by the arm and led us to the town where they all lived. It was like a parade when we walked into the town followed by hundreds of people. The thing was, the more we walked, the more people jumped into the crowd. At the end of the "parade" we were placed on a set of thrones and a huge number of offerings were made to us.

We partied until the moons were well above us. Pandorica had tried to refuse the plentiful wine offered, but our enthusiastic worshippers looked so upset every time she refused, she soon relented and accepted all the food, drink and gifts that were offered and we both eventually were taken to a room that had been prepared for us, and we both lay down on the luxurious tent like bed, kissed ardently, and then passed out.

ENTRY 31
09.04.63.23.32


The party lasted for two days, and Pandorica and I danced for so long that we were exhausted by the time everything wound down, and everyone went home.

We found a nice quiet place and settled down to sleep and relax together, but it did not last very long, it is now 15 hours later and they are all constantly asking for my help. God, I hate being a god!

The first thing I had to do was to baptize a number of the by now slightly inebriated adult worshipers. I decided that instead of dunking them,  from what I remembered they did back home, I decided to make it much more enjoyable for them and so, instead, I gave them a ceremonial shot of very, very strong alcohol.

Naturally, they acted even more strangely afterward, especially towards me, their new god, bowing and stuff like that, but I must admit it was so enjoyable watching them stumbling around admiring me, I could do nothing wrong. The way I figured if that is what they believed me to be, then I was going to have some fun while I could.

Then it was marriages. I had five weddings to do. Now, I did them all as  straight as I could, but half of the grooms were really loaded and I doubted that they would even remember the ceremony, yet they all wanted it, so I did it.

Dinner was the best I have ever eaten, since I suddenly found myself on Zartoon. We had roasted meats, wine, exotic fruits and vegetables and some kind of Zartoon chocolate. It wasn't as good at home, but hey, it was chocolate so I enjoyed it just as much as I would have back home.

After the meal, some of the young females came up to me and offered their bodies to me. Of course, I declined the offers, since I was involved romantically with Pandorica, but I never explained that to them. So, since I wouldn't take their bodies, they then generously offered to be my wives instead. Now, what on Zartoon would I do with fifteen wives? No, I said to each and every one of them. Then I made an announcement that I really did think about. I didn't ask about it, I just did it. "I would like to make an announcement," I said to the crowd. "From this day forward, Pandorica and I are married, and I will accept no other wives."

Pandorica didn't react to the announcement in any way. I can only guess that she felt that we were already married, and yeah, that was perfectly fine with me.

The last thing I did today as a God, was to serve as a judge on a case of burglary. A man stole a wooden chalice from a shop. He explained that he didn't steal it... he was just borrowing to give some water to his wife. I stood up, to announce my decision. Naturally,

I did not want to sentence this man to jail. It would not fit the crime, so instead I ordered him to work a full shift at the shop to pay for the chalice he had borrowed.

The crowd went berserk to say that least. This was the first time that a citizen was not killed for the smallest of crimes. "The old god was very vengeful," one of the men told me. "You are a blessing to this land and its people."

After that I went into my room and shut the door behind me. Pandorica was lying naked on the bed. For the first time, making love to her felt right... in fact perfect would be a better word! I was in for the night with the woman I loved and that was all this god wanted!

ENTRY 32
11.04.63.08.55

In the morning, I called the council together to tell them that I had to leave, just temporarily. When I told them this news, all of them echoed the same sentiment, that I couldn't leave... not at that time. They said that their land was in great turmoil, and that I was the only person holding it together.

So I then told them that it was a command from their eternal father and that I would not be gone long. That seemed to calm their fears a lot, but they were still reluctant to see me leave.

I gathered together two travelers and Pandorica, and I left for the Zartoon city. Their motors were rough, and it took some time to get them started, but once they caught they roared into action. At first it felt like we were riding a mustang, but it calmed to a purring kitten within seconds.

It was a long trip, but it was a lot faster than it would have been walking or traveling by animal, so we did have time for me to stop and visit some friends on the way back. I rode into the "hippie" village and they recognized me as soon as I pulled in. Pandorica and I were surrounded by friends and we both received all the kisses we could handle and more.

"We have missed you my friend," one of them said.

"I am glad to be back," I replied. Then I told them that Pandorica was now my wife. Then I got a shock, I am still not yet over.

One of the women walked over to Pandorica and placed her hand on her stomach. "Congratulations Pandorica," the woman said. "It will not be long"

"What won't be long?" Pandorica asked with more curiosity than she should have.

"The birth of your child," the woman said as she smiled and hugged Pandorica.

"How?" I asked as I starting going into shock. One of the men laughed and explained the facts of life to me. "I know HOW it happened, but we only...!!!" Then I realized that it only takes once, and certainly we had certainly made love more than once, in fact, we already did have a son, but that first child was different, there was no love between us at that time, but now it was so different, so I just sat down and stared into the fire. Another egg would soon hatch, but this time it was so different, this time it meant so much more to me.

One of the men brought me over a bottle of something they called alcohol. Humans wouldn't call it that, but he did. It was a huge bottle and it tasted like shit, but it did its job and, within a couple minutes I was drunk as hell. It wasn't that I was sad or anything like that. I was happy, I did love Pandorica, but I was also in a state of shock, and getting drunk seemed to be the best way to relieve that feeling.

Pandorica was escorted to a hut with a nice soft bed but me.... I was left to pass out by the fire, and I did.

## ENTRY 33
12.04.63.14.35


We left our friends early this morning and continued on our journey to the Zartoon city. It was still a long way off, but with our travelers I knew we could make it before night came. It would be hard, but we could make it. It was strange though, nothing happened for a few hours, but then we hit a storm. We saw it coming over the flat ground miles away, so immediately Pandorica and I found a deep ditch we could hide in.

We talked through the storm when we were able to hear each other over the wind. Now, this is just a guess, but I would say that the winds were either equal to or more than a level 5 hurricane. We were down fairly deep in that ditch, but we saw animals, bushes and even trees flying overhead. God, were we lucky that we were safe.

"How do you feel about the baby?" Pandorica asked. I wasn't going to lie to her. It was a shock and I think that she understood that.. Maybe it might have been a shock to her as well, and I also was wondering what her father would say. This wasn't a situation like before when Pandorica had been ordered to my bed.

This was a child born of love, one that had not been  pre-ordered by the Zartoon council. Maybe it wouldn't be too bad since we are married, but then again… who knew how a Zartoon father would react to, not a male hatchling this time, but a child born of love, between his daughter and Fa Nex, the human from Phoenix?

"Pandorica, I am so happy for us," I said. Well, I couldn't hurt her feelings could I, and I really was happy. "I am looking forward to being a father to a child born of our love!" She smiled and looked so happy, and relieved, possibly my getting drunk so quickly the night before might have made her slightly apprehensive.

Now I could see she was content and happy. "It will be different this time Fa Nex" she whispered softly, "so very different. A child born of true feelings between a Zartoon and a human, is a very different type of birth, to the one that produced our son." She looked at me with a softness in her eyes that I found so beautiful. "This will be a birth, more like a human birth of your world, Fa Nex. I do not why this is, but it just is." she smiled knowingly as the storm raged above us. "It has happened many times before when a Zartoon and a human mated in love, and not just in authorized reproduction.

This time, it will be an actual human birthing, not just a Zartoon hatching of an egg." I did not reply, and even though this horrific storm was raging above us, I felt calm and at peace and so overcome with feelings for Pandorica and our child.

The storm passed after an hour, and we

were back on the trip again. There was nobody to be seen along the way. Even the Human patrols were strangely missing, but certainly we had no intention to stop at the Human city to find out what was going on. We actually went a few miles out of the way to make sure we didn't get too close to the city.

Finally, we were within sight of the Zartoon city.

"There is something wrong," Pandorica said so we both dropped to the ground and got as low to the ground as we could. "Look," she said as she pointed above the city. There were extremely large birds flying over the Zartoon city.

I had never seen anything like them before, but Pandorica had and she was not happy to see them now. "Those birds are called Mystical Eagles and they only show up when something has gone seriously wrong. I have seen them before, but never that many in one place."

We watched as the birds flew around, occasionally diving behind the city walls. There had to have been something wrong, very wrong indeed. We decided that it would be better to enter the city after dark. The birds would be long gone and it would be safer for us so we just sat and waited, but I have also taken time out to write this entry. Now I have to rest up till tonight, when we will together as husband and wife return to the Zartoon city and Pandorica's family.

That night, Pandorica and I started walking to her city. It was really quiet. There were no sounds of the ships that used to patrol the area. There were no sounds of children coming from just outside the wall, and there were no sounds of normal life anywhere to be found.

We got to the city's gate and there was no one there. We didn't pause to think, we just ran into the city, and there was no one anywhere. There were no signs of a battle, no bodies, nothing whatsoever. As we walked, I looked into each of the buildings. There were clothes, cooking tools and food still left on the tables, and the fireplaces were stocked for a night's warmth, and I even saw a few pets sitting by their bowls looking for someone to feed them.

"What in the hell happened here," I asked Pandorica who had disappeared from my side. I had a feeling where she went so I followed her and I was right... she went to the palace. Like the other buildings, it looked as if everyone just disappeared without any kind of warning.

"Where is everybody," Pandorica asked. She was starting to cry and no matter what I did, she would not, maybe could not, calm down. "My family... they are all gone!" I had never seen her so emotional, so I sat her down, gave her a kiss, and then I came up with an idea.

I'd climb one of the towers of the palace and see what was in the area. I couldn't get her to sit still so I let her follow me.

The tower was high, with so many steps that my legs were burning when I finally reached the top. We both looked around all the way out to the horizon. It took a little while, but Pandorica finally saw very faint tracks leading from the back gate of the city out into a desert just west of the city. We rushed back down the tower. My legs were still burning from the climb, and let me tell you, my legs were nearly falling off when we got to the bottom.

Once we got out of the gate we saw thousands of footprints. Men's, women's and children's, they were all leading away from town. There were even tracks of sleds and travelers. Going by the depth of the tracks, they were traveling quite fast and it looked like each one was carrying a number of passengers... more than the travelers were designed to carry.

"They all left the city," Pandorica said. "They all just up and left!"

I tried to figure out what would cause an entire city to leave in such a hurry, but not one idea I had made any sense but, then again, none of this made any sense.

I noticed that Pandorica was showing a lot of fatigue so I took her into her house and put her to bed. Me, I didn't sleep right away. I wanted to check out the area more to maybe see something, anything that might give me an answer. I will sleep later if I get the chance, but now, I am going to walk around the wall. I will report more when/if I find something.

## ENTRY 35
14.04.63.19.35

I didn't get any sleep last night and I doubt that Pandorica got much either The city was actually very spooky. I hate to use the word, but it is the only one that fits. The winds made such unbelievable sounds, as if there were ghosts wandering the streets and buildings.

After we ate, we went and searched some of the buildings. In one of them, near the palace, we found a stash of weapons. I grabbed two blasters and two pistols. After all, God only knew what we would find once we left. Then we found a supply of food and water. It would have been enough for the city to survive for years if their normal supply disappeared, and it was all still there. A stock list on the door showed that everything that should have been there was there. "Why didn't they take any?" I said, but Pandorica didn't have an answer either. So we just gathered up some of the food and water and made our way down to the city's rear gate.

It was easy to open, but when I did I saw exactly what I didn't want to see. There had been a windstorm during the night and all of the tracks that we saw the day before were gone... buried under fresh sand. There was some good news, though, both Pandorica and I both remembered which way the tracks went, so we just decided to travel in that direction. Unfortunately, we have not taken our travelers with us since the ones we were using were low on fuel and there were no others in the city so it was going to be a very long walk.

Usually the Zartoon air was cool... maybe fifty to sixty degrees, but today it was hot and it was very thick. That made the traveling harder than it had been. We only covered about twenty miles when we had to sit down and rest. We were exhausted, hungry, and thirsty. Honestly though, I didn't care about me, I was worried about Pandorica. Besides everything else, she had the stress of being pregnant, and I had no idea what this was doing to her and our baby.

Then I had a stroke of the purest luck, I have ever had. I smelled something sweet in the air. It was kind of like a cross between caramel and roses, and it was coming from over a dune a couple of miles away. We rested for about an hour before we walked to where the smell was coming from.

It was like something I had never seen before... even here on Zartoon. There was an oasis. It was covered with a thick fog. Inside of the fog there were trees with large red leaves and purple fruits. I found the flowers that made such an incredible smell. They were small, about the size of the head of a pin, yellow, and so beautiful. I went to pick one to give to Pandorica but the minute I touched it, my finger got burnt, burnt so bad that it immediately developed blisters.

Pandorica was sitting in a field of grass. I ran up and grabbed her by the arm. "Honey, do not touch anything here," I said. "I don't know what is poisonous and what isn't." She promised me that she wouldn't, then she just rolled over and went to sleep. Despite the pain in my finger, I decided I was going to do exactly the same thing.

ENTRY 36
15.04.63.08.35

Pandorica and I just woke up. My hand is completely swollen and has begun to turn blue, the pain is totally unbearable, and she has no idea on how to help me. It is so horrendous that I am pretty sure that I am going to die fairly shortly, but I cannot, will not let her know how concerned I am for my health.

I asked her if she had ever heard of anything like the oasis we were in. "I had heard stories about islands in the great sea where the plants and animals are poisonous. We have been banned from there since time immemorial. There was one who went there a year ago and he never came back. That just reinforced the ban and scared us all into never trying it again, but I have never heard of anything like that on land."

That was bad... really bad but that wasn't the worst news. Winds during the night had erased our own footprints so we had no idea where to go ahead and no idea exactly where we had come from so it was going be just dead reckoning and the hope we got it at least somewhat right.

I really couldn't travel, but I didn't want to endanger Pandorica so I looked at the sun and we started walking with the sun to our back. In my mind, it was much safer to be walking than it would be if Pandorica happened to touch the wrong plant.

## ENTRY 37
15.04.63.23.58

I am sorry… so sorry for Pandorica and our baby. My arm is blue all of the way up past the elbow, and I am starting to feel it all over the rest of my body. I am getting so weak, Pandorica found a valley for me to rest in. I do not want to die, I want to see my son or daughter when it's born. Pandorica is over sitting on a half rotten log, and right now she is bawling her eyes out.

Then, suddenly, she stopped crying and instead got angry… angrier than I had ever seen her before. I was lying on the ground, writhing in pain. She then walked over to me pulled my arm out to the side, placed her foot on my wrist and pressed down as hard as she could. The pain was so intense there was no way I should have been able to stand it, but I did.

She pulled one of the rifles out from behind her and fired into my shoulder. I passed out right after that, at least I think I must have, because I woke up just a little while ago. I was still in pain, but now my shoulder was all bandaged up.

The most important thing of all, I was still alive. Then I looked, and saw that Pandorica was lying right beside me, keeping me warm with her body. Unfortunately, I also saw that my arm was blown off a few inches below the shoulder, and the sand all around me was soaked with my blood.

Just then, Pandorica opened her eyes, leaned over and kissed me, and then she told me that I was not allowed to die... not for a long time to come.

I am very, very tired and I feel like I am going to pass out again, so I want to get this recorded before I forget any of it. If I am still alive, I will record more later.

ENTRY 38
16.04.63.13.13


I woke up and I wondered what in the hell happened. The start of the night I was in a lot of pain, it was so bad that I cried in Pandorica's arms. I was so happy that she was there, I doubt that I could have made it through if it wasn't for her. Like I said, the night started out with a lot of pain, but as the night went on, it changed from pain into an intense tingling. It felt as if my arm was asleep, but I thought, maybe, it was the phantom limbs I heard about when people lose an arm or leg. Anyway, I finally got to sleep just before the sun came up.

"Fa Nex," Pandorica yelled as the sun got just over the horizon. "Look!"

I looked down and I saw something I could not believe. Where she had shot my arm off the night before was the start of new, fresh, pink flesh. It looked like the arm of a newborn baby, but it was definitely an arm. Hell, it even had five fingers. "I was hoping that would happen," she said.

"Hoping what would happen," I asked

"There was only one moon last night, did you see that?" she asked. I said that I had noticed that. "Our two moons lined up one behind the other. The Yartook... they fear those nights. They hide in their homes because the radiation from the moons is stronger than any other nights. We have known for generations that it is a healing night, and it worked on your arm, just as I thought it would."

"How many times does this happen?" I asked. She told me that it happens two or three times a year.

"We have gotten to where we can predict its occurrence and we take full use of it," she said with a smile. "We plant on those nights. The plants grow bigger and stronger when the two moons join in the sky." I could understand that, somewhat, but there were still some questions I needed Pandorica to answer, but not for now.

By midday, my arm was almost totally healed. I could move it, and my fingers, as easily as I could before, and there was no more pain or tingling. Hell, there wasn't even a scar to speak of. I rested another hour before we decided to start walking.

We had no idea which way to go, so I made the decision to use a tool that olden days pilots used to find their way… dead reckoning. If it worked, we'd be fine… if not, we were going to be in trouble. I will let you know later today what happened.

## ENTRY 39
18.04.63.23.13

The moons are directly above us. We had been walking for two days now… our supplies are running low, and we were lucky we found a place with a lot of water yesterday, but there weren't any plants that we could have been able to eat. I have been giving Pandorica most of my food. She needs it more than I do, I don't want anything to happen to her or the baby.

One thing we found this morning were the remains of some ancient town. It was mostly just stones, and some very roughly carved tiles. There were carvings on the wall, but they were not in the Zartoon language. They were pictographs and, from what I could decipher, what they were saying was good. I think it talked about their last days before the Sane came in and took over their town, still that was long ago, and nothing they said back then was going to do us any good. There was one other thing in that town, we found food containers from Pandorica's village. Despite the fact that there were no tracks, instantly I knew that her people had been through that town and that we were on the right course.

There was a large sand dune in front of us, and it was not the rocky sand we had been used to. It was loose, grainy sand that would be nearly impossible to walk through. My thoughts went back to the travelers we had so long ago, it would have been no trouble to make it up the one side and down the other if only we had been able to ride.

I really still wasn't feeling well, but I took Pandorica by the hand and led her onto the dune. It was hot and drier than anything we hand experienced before. I could feel my lips cracking as we climbed, yeah, I did have some water, but I gave it to Pandorica as I wanted it to last as long as possible. Pandorica and the baby, they were all that mattered at that moment.

It took us over an hour to climb the dune. My hands and knees were bloody and Pandorica's were not much better! So, when we reached the top and started down the opposite side, we just sat down and slid down the dune, just like I did as a kid whenever it snowed. To tell the truth, that was the most fun we had since we left the temple.

At the bottom of the dune was a small stream that we decided to follow, and we were lucky that we did. A couple of hours from the dune, we found a small group of plants with rather large insects flying around them. They looked a lot like the dragonflies from back home. Now, the plants couldn't be eaten, but the insects were a different story. Pandorica and I both caught and ate our fill, they didn't taste all that great, but they were good.

We were semi-refreshed, but we were not going to stop. Pandorica said that she saw some faint traces of smoke coming from not too far away so we started walking in that direction. It wasn't far before could see a very large campsite. There were fires and the smell of food filled the air. Pandorica's ears perked up as if she could hear something that I couldn't.

"Father," she yelled as she ran into the campsite. It was almost a miracle, we had actually found her people on a planet that is covered with miles and miles of nothing.

I followed her and she led me directly to her father. "Father, this is Fa Nex," she said. He told her that he remembered me. Then she told him that I was her husband and that she was pregnant. I did not get the response I expected from him, instead of yelling he hugged me and wished us both luck.

Later he held a party for the entire camp. There was food and drink... music and dancing. It was all in celebration of Pandorica and I. It lasted well into the night and, as soon as we could get away, we started to fall asleep in the sand, but I wanted to record this before I slept... just in case I forgot anything.

You know, if you didn't know better, you'd swear that the campsite they set up was just their old city without the buildings or the walls. They were living exactly the way they were when I first met them. Hell, even Pandorica fit right back into her old routine, except I will admit she spent much more time in the nursery than she ever did before. The important thing was, she was enjoying being with her family, and so that made me happy.

I had slept late, and I awoke to find my Pandorica long gone as I went to pick up my bag to go and find her, but two guards came into our shelter. One grabbed one arm and the other grabbed my other arm, they also grabbed my bag, then I was held as they searched me, and then handed me back the bag and took me directly to their Zartoon leader.

"Where is the sword?" he demanded excitedly as soon as I walked into the room. I immediately reached into my bag and brought the sword out and handed it to the leader.

"Fa Nex, you have done an incredible thing for our people and you will always be one of us as long as the Zartoon survive on this world."

I thanked him as I watched him run his finger up the edge of the blade. Then, all of a sudden his cheer turned into sadness. "Fa Nex, there is something wrong with this sword."

"There can't be," I said. "I found it in a cave beneath a temple and I had a hard time getting it with the guards. In fact Pandorica had to retrieve it because she had a pure spirit. Otherwise, we would never be allowed to have it."

"Its power is gone," he said with a deep sadness in his eyes. "It should have glowed brighter than the sun when my blood touched it. There is something wrong and I don't understand."

Just then the Zartoon religious leader walked up to us. "I know what is wrong," he said to the his leader. "It was buried for too long." Then he ordered us to look closely at the blade. When we did, we saw a line of black traveling up from the hilt to the tip. It was narrower than the width of a Human hair, but it was there. "I do not believe that this sword has been purified in many centuries. It needs to feel the waters of the waterfall in Nifero Haarth."

"What is that?" I asked.

"The Yartook call that area Warrego Valles," the religious leader said. Then he told me just what I thought he was going to say. "Since the sword chose Pandorica as its guardian, Pandorica has to be the one to purify the sword."

At first I was reluctant to agree because of her pregnancy, but they assured me that the trip would not be hard and she would be more than able to make it there and back before the baby was due.

I didn't tell her, anything about this yet. I wanted her to have this day to enjoy life. Tomorrow would be good enough. Then I walked over to the nursery and spent the rest of the day watching her play with the babies. Like I said ... tomorrow will be another day.

## ENTRY 41
## 20.04.63.12.03

For the first time in a very long time, I was afraid to wake up next to Pandorica. I didn't want to, but I knew I had to tell her that we had to leave again. I remember that right after she woke up, I asked her why her people left their city for such a desolate place.

"I was told that a hot wind blew in from the desert. It was hotter than it had ever been, and all of the foodstuffs and water turned to dust, so unless they left, there would not have been a city to return to."

"Did you tell them that we passed through there and everything was fine?" I asked.

Pandorica said that she had told them that, and that they had immediately sent two scouts out to see if what she was saying was true. "My father told me that if they find the city environmentally safe, then they will return and settle the area again," she said with a smile. But her smile faded as I told her that our mission was not over yet.

"We have to go to Warrego Valles and purify the sword," I said. "I do not know where that is or how far it is, but I guess, Pandorica, we have to go." She said she knew where it was and it was a very, very long way away. As Pandorica was pregnant, this was a real worry, what in the hell, I thought, isn't there anything close by on this damn planet?

Pandorica of course went and said goodbye to everyone, explaining we would be back soon. Me, I just waved, and we started out.

Once again, there was no road and not even a path. It was nothing but sand, and sagebrush, but this time we were smart. I grabbed a bunch of the dehydrated foods that they had stored in a tent at the edge of the camp. I also managed to get a pretty good supply of water, so we would definitely be able to eat and drink on the way.

Pandorica told me how beautiful the waterfall was that we were going to. "The water is so blue and cold, but my husband, the light from the sky makes it look this beautiful violet color. There are rocks on the side of the falls where you can dive. I love watching the Zartoon dive into the water. They are so graceful. It is almost like seeing music as a solid form. There are so many plants and flowers that it looked as if the gods painted the whole area."

"Then you have been there," I asked.

"Just in my dreams," Pandorica said. "In my dreams I have been there a thousand times and I loved every one of them."

It was so romantic sounding and still I was disappointed. I just wanted to get there as quickly as possible... partly to get the mission over and done with and partly to give Pandorica her dream.

I am going to end this because Pandorica looks like she needs me to love her. Leaving her family again must have been hard on her. I will record more later.

ENTRY 42
20.04.63.20.03

There is one good thing. Today the air was cool and I could smell the distinct smell of salt, which was strange since the nearest water was more than two days behind us and, as far as I knew, the closest sea was even further than that. Now, I am not one who questions blessings, but that was a little too much to just accept.

Pandorica got over her disappointment of leaving her family and was now actually looking forward to making the trip. I guess all it took was for her to find out where we were going to make her happy. The only thing I am concerned with about her is that she is starting to show. Now, I don't know how long the gestation period is for a Zartoon and human mating, but I am sure that it isn't the nine months human pregnancies are.

Night came a couple of hours ago and Pandorica didn't want to stop walking, even after we couldn't see a foot in front of us, but I finally talked her into resting, after I told that if she didn't, she would not be able to enjoy the falls when we got to them. So, I picked some scrub brush, built a fire and we decided to make love and then get some sleep under the Zartoon moons.

ENTRY 43
20.04.63.13.53

We traveled about five hours already today. Amazingly the air was still cool despite the fact that we were in the desert. Suddenly, there was a valley before us. It was deep and had vertical walls that must have dropped more than fifty feet, and I saw that it reached for miles in either direction. Somehow we had to get down there, but at the bottom I could see water. It was dark and totally smooth, but it has been watered just the same.

"Pandorica," I said. "We are going to have to jump. When we do jump spread your arms and legs as far apart as they will go. It will slow our fall and I am sure that we will be alright when we land at the bottom." She looked at me as if I was nuts or worse but she trusted me and, besides that, we had no other way to go. "Three... two... one," I counted as I grabbed her hand and we both went over the edge of the cliff. I was right, we fell even slower than I expected, so when we hit the water we both went under about ten feet, thankfully we came right back up, and when we did we just started drifting.

I don't know how far we went or how long it was but when we rounded one of the corners, of which there were many, we saw a village carved into the side of the cliff. We could see Zartoon all through the rock's openings. Males, females, and children, all living their idyllic lives. There were some out on the river fishing and a number of boats tied to the side of the cliff. I grabbed Pandorica and we swam over to a dock that stuck out into the river.

As soon as we lifted ourselves out of the water we were surrounded by at least a dozen of the males from the village. Immediately, they took Pandorica by the arm and led her into the village. *They must not get many visitors,* I thought, but then I noticed that they had left me, dripping wet, standing on the dock. However, one male walked down to meet me. "What is your name," he asked.

"I am Williams from Phoenix," I replied just as I did when I was asked before.

"Williams From Phoenix," he said. "Welcome to the land of the Tergina."

I stuck my hand out to shake his but all he did was back away as if I had the plague or something like that. "That is a sign of friendship where I come from," I said as he reluctantly shook my hand.

"Where is it that you are from Williams from Phoenix," he asked.

You know, I didn't know if that was better than Fa Nex or not, but at least it was partially right. That made me smile a little. "I am from a world called Yartook," I replied.

"I have heard of that world," he said as he started walking me into the village. "I always thought that it was just a myth that

112

grandmothers told to little ones." I assured him that it was no myth. It was dying, but it was not a myth by any means. As we stepped into the village, he put his hands to his mouth and yelled, "Yesat huej hythe Yartook kterf Williams From Phoenix!" As soon as he said that a roar came from all of the people around. They were chanting "Williams From Phoenix" over and over again.

I just stood there for a minute thinking again how this place obviously didn't get many visitors to be this excited to see a poor boy from Phoenix, Arizona. I really didn't mind, though, it was kind of fun. After all of the commotion calmed down I asked to go look for Pandorica. But I didn't have long to look.

They brought her out and she was dressed in the finest gown made of gold and covered with thousands of gemstones, and the minute she stepped onto a small platform everyone turned to face her and they all dropped to their knees. One of the males came running over to me and knocked my knees out from beneath me. "You have to bow to her," he commanded.

I just laid on the ground confused. I had no idea what was going on. Why was she dressed like that and why did everyone bow to her?

As quickly as she came out, she was taken again. She looked directly at me, but she didn't say a word. She was taken one way and I was taken another. I had no idea what they had done to her or where she was going and no one told me anything. It is all very strange, but I guess I just have to sit and wait.

## ENTRY 44
## 21.04.63.18.53


I finally got to see Pandorica. She was so dressed up and perfumed that I could not understand what was going on with her, then just before I had the chance to say anything someone walked in and whisked her out again.

"Pandorica," I yelled. "What's going on?" Just then someone else came in and he started talking to me.

"How do you know her," he asked. I explained that we had been traveling together since I met her in her city and she followed me on a mission that her people sent me on. "You should be very honored. It is not common for a female such as her to associate with someone like you."

"A female like her" I asked with a very sarcastic voice. I didn't care at that moment if he heard it or not. I was getting really pissed.

"The female you call Pandorica is not who you think she is," he said. "Her name is Gavabu and she is the crown princess of the Zartoon home world." I denied it of course, that was ridiculous, but he kept on insisting that she was indeed the princess and he would not hear any more of it, but he certainly did hear when I said that Pandorica and I were married and that she was expecting a baby.

Once he heard that he dropped to his knees,

bowing to me and asking my forgiveness…
which of course I gave. Then he asked my
permission to leave, which I granted.

A few minutes later, he returned with
Pandorica and three or four others. She told
them yes, indeed we were married and that
she was expecting my baby. I don't know what
happened, but suddenly I was taken from my
room and led through the building to a room
that was fancy by anyone's standards.

"Prince Fa Nex," one of them said as they
sat me on a chair. "We had no idea that you are
Her Highness's husband. We offer you our city
and everything we have." I thanked them and
told them that all I wanted was to see Pandorica
alone so we could talk. "I will ask Her Highness,
if she would like to see you," one of them said
just as he left the room.

I was left alone and I had a lot to figure out
so I just sat there looking at the furniture, the
river below and the patterns on the cliff across
the way. Other than all of that, I just waited.

You know that was a lot to take in. Pandorica a princess? Why didn't she tell me who she was? I told one of the Zartoon who were taking care of me that I wanted to see her, and I wanted to see her right then! That was easier than I thought it was going to be. He went off and a few minutes later he returned and said that I was granted and audience with her highness, but it was only going to be for a few minutes. I didn't like it, but I agreed.

The area Pandorica was staying in wasn't as grandiose as any princess would have demanded back on Earth. It was sparse to say the least, but I could tell that someone important was there. Her door had two guards standing in front of it. They looked meaner than any bouncers I had ever seen.

My escorts dropped back as I approached the door. One of the guards searched me. I guess they were afraid that maybe I wanted to kill her or something like that, but  naturally knew that was never going to happen. I loved her, and happily I know that Pandorica knew that too.

Finally, I got to see her. She had at least twenty ladies-in-waiting. I could not believe it. She had everything that she could possibly want.

"Your Highness," I said as I walked over

and took her in my arms. "I am very honored to meet you."

"Fa Nex," she said with an embarrassed smile. "Please do not ever call me that." She kissed me and it was the same loving kiss we had shared so many times before.

"Who is Gavabu," I asked.

"She died so many cycles ago," Pandorica replied. "I did not like who she was becoming so I denounced the crown and I became a simple girl named Pandorica. I like her so much better." I told her that I liked Pandorica better too. That made her so happy. I went over and whispered something in her ear and, as soon as I did, she commanded everyone in the room to leave. Then she locked the door behind them, disrobed in a very sexy fashion and we walked to the bed. That night we made love until the early hours of the morning and then I was escorted back to my room where I recorded this. I hope I can see her again tomorrow. I really do miss her.

## ENTRY 46
22.04.63.19.23

Pandorica came to my room about a couple hours ago. That was actually quite a shock, but what she had to say was more of a shock. She wanted to leave this kingdom of hers and she wanted to leave immediately! She had decided, so many cycles ago, she wanted no part of being a princess. I was so relieved she felt that way, as I had been having the same feelings ever since my first day here. We talked about it for a while and together we came up with an idea. She kissed me and then called her guards and they escorted her back to her royal chambers.

A few hours later as the sun started going down, as we had planned, I went out on the edge of the ledge. There were several boats tied in the river directly below me. It was just a minute or two after I got there when Pandorica walked up with her escorts. "Leave me," she ordered her escorts. "I want to spend time with my husband once again with no one around." When they refused to leave, she reminded them who she was and demanded that they leave or face her wrath. She stood with her eyes locked on them as they turned and went into one of the nearby buildings.

"Let's go," I said to her as I took her hand and we started climbing down the face of the cliff.

We made it down without any problems. Once we were safe on the river, I took a log from the shoreline and punched holes into the bottom of every boat except one. That one we climbed in and started once again to drift down the river and toward Warrego Valles. As we drifted away, I could hear voices calling for Princess Gavabu and calling for guards to search the city and the area to find out where she went. Thankfully, they were not going to find her. It was too dark for them to see into the valley and, even if they could, there was no way for them to follow us, so we just lay back in the boat and relaxed as the city faded into the distance.

ENTRY 47
23.04.63.02.07


We drifted for a couple of hours before we heard, anything other than some of the birds that flew above the ridge of the canyon. Then another noise came from in front of us. I knew the sound from the times I visited Niagara Falls when I was a kid. It was the roar of a waterfall and going by the loudness it was a big one. Since we were drifting toward the sound that meant that we were on the top of the falls and would be going over if we didn't do anything.

"Pandorica," I said in a voice that showed just a bit of panic. "Do you know anything about this canyon or the way the river is going to go?"

"I have never been here," she said. "There are no legends about it and no one I know has ever been here."

The walls of the canyon were as smooth as glass so there was nowhere to dock the boat and now the water was moving a lot faster than it had been when we started. I could feel rocks hitting the bottom of the boat as they tore shards of wood from the hull. There were a couple of small holes torn into the bottom of the boat. I used my hands to cover them and stop the water from coming in.

It was no more than a few minutes later when Pandorica saw a mist coming from around the bend in the river. The roar was so loud that we couldn't have heard each other if our lives had depended on it. Then there it was... a massive waterfall more than 300 feet high and it was falling directly in front of us. The thing was it was not falling from the river we were on. It was falling into the river from a giant stone wall directly in front of us.

It seemed impossible, but the water was not coming at us from the falls... we were headed into the waterfall.

Finally, we reached the edge of the waterfall. I was right. The river went underneath the waterfall and into a cave. We were pounded by the water as we passed through. Pandorica got onto her hands and knees as she tried to protect herself and the baby. But, even in that position she took one hell of a beating. Me, I had seen bodies of some people who went over waterfalls so I was praying to my God, the Zartoon gods, and cursing the planet at the same time that we three would make it through alive and safe.

The boat rocked so violently that the keel was out of the water and the boat nearly flipped over several times. Again and again we were smashed into rocks and sandbars. I was afraid that we would be trapped by the raging water, but then, as quickly as it started, it was over.

The cave where the river flowed was wider than any other part of the canyon had ever been, so the boat drifted calmly on the water. There was light coming from the opening where we had just entered and another light from an opening far off in the distance. We were going to be alright so I whispered into Pandorica's ear that I loved her and I was so happy she was safe. Then we both watched the light ahead of us and we relaxed, even though who knew what awaited us when we did get there, but for now... and thanking all the Gods, the worse was over.

ENTRY 48
23.04.63.08.50


We made it out of the cave a few hours ago. It was so nice to see the light of the moons once again. It was going good until Pandorica screamed for me to get to shore immediately! She was yelling and crying so I found the first clear area and pulled the boat onto the sand. Pandorica ran onto the beach and started digging. It wasn't a deep hole just enough to hold her. I tried to help but she turned on me with her eyes glazed over and her teeth bared so I just decided to back off.

Honestly I was planning on stopping anyway to rest for the night, but I had no idea it was going to be like that.

I walked over to Pandorica and asked her if I could do anything to help and she raised her hand to me. Her claws were out and I had the idea that she was more than willing to use them if I got any closer.

"Are you alright," I asked.

"Fa Nex," she growled. "Back off or I swear to the gods of Zartoon I will tear your head from your shoulders." Then she let out a scream that I knew could be heard all the way to Earth and back. "I am warning you back away or I will not be able to protect you much longer!"

I decided that this was not a battle that I could ever have hope of winning, so I told her that I loved her and then went to the other side of the beach and just sat there. I could hear her screaming and crying, but believe me there was no way I was going to go anywhere near her until she called for me... no matter how long that took.

I had no idea what was happening... Well, to tell the truth, I did have an idea of what was happening, but I couldn't be sure how rough it would be. After an hour I heard some rocks smashing while she threw others into the deepest part of the river. She was also cursing at me, the Zartoon gods, her mother and father, and even the red sky above. At that moment I was sorry that I drank that liquid that allowed me to understand her. Then, suddenly she went quiet. I mean, it was way too quiet.

"Fa Nex," she called out. "Come to me!" Now, I didn't know if it was a trap or what but I decided to go anyway, but her voice sounded pretty much the way it always had... cheerful and friendly so I figured that I might be safe after all. As I moved closer I saw her sitting back against a rock. She was smiling and cooing. It was then I knew that she had given birth to our baby.

"Is that...," I started to ask.

"Fa Nex, come and meet your daughter," Pandorica said with a smile. She was holding a little girl that some would consider a monster, but to me she was just as perfect as she could ever be. Her hair was the most beautiful shade of blue and she had the eyes of her mother. Her skin was a soft pink and completely flawless. Even the few scales she had were beautiful shades of pastel green with tints of gold. I could not have been prouder of her. "I would like her named after my grandmother is that is alright with you?" Pandorica asked, I told her that I would be honored if she did so.

After holding our baby daughter in my arms and making sure Pandorica was aware just how much I loved her. Safe on dry land, and feeling utterly content at that moment, Pandorica, Rhosly and I settled in for the next couple of days... our first days together as a family.

ENTRY 49
25.04.63.17.27


Rhosly is doing well, I have never seen a baby grow so fast, still that could be the Zartoon DNA from her mother kicking in. I mean she's only two days old and she has already doubled in size and God is she beautiful. She still has the beauty of Pandorica in her, but I can now also see more of me coming out in her with every passing hour. It is so incredible.

Today we caught some fish out of the river for breakfast, loaded everything and everyone into the boat and started out again on our journey. We were lucky. The air was cool enough for the baby to be comfortable and there was a gentle breeze coming from in front of us so we had good traveling for the next few miles.

The cliffs finally smoothed down to where we were looking out at the plains that seemed to go on forever and a day. In the distance I could see tall flowering trees with large birds flying around them. The clouds were the strangest shade of violet I had ever seen. It was really quite beautiful, and I just sat back and relaxed as we drifted along. Pandorica was too busy to see any of these things. Rhosly was hungry and she was sure going to let everybody on Zartoon know about it. Our little girl was already mature enough to eat solid food, so Pandorica reached into the water and grabbed a fish that happened to be swimming close to the surface. It wasn't that big of a fish so Rhosly ate it with no problem.

It was another few miles before we came upon an abandoned building. "That is the Temple of the Sun," Pandorica said. "That religion died out so long ago that there is little known about them except their symbol." She pointed at an eighteen pointed star over the front door of the building. "They are famous for killing anyone who intruded into their world. It would not be a good place for us to stop!"

You know that was the one thing she should never have said. When people tell me NOT to go somewhere, that is when I go, so I pulled the boat to shore and beached it. Pandorica and Rhosly stayed in the boat, but I decided to see what I could see. The second my foot hit the ground, it changed into a liquid and formed around my shoe. It became hard and, once it began to heat up, I decided that it was time for this country boy to get his ass out of there. I grabbed a nearby rock and started chipping away at my prison. Finally, I must have hit it in just the right spot because it shattered into dust. I pulled my foot back, jumped into the boat and we were gone. I was okay except for the fact that my shoe was dirty, but that was no big deal.

We just kept drifting and playing with the baby the rest of the day until we finally saw Warrego Valles in the distance. We wanted to go in in the morning so we set up camp on the shore. Rhosly hopped out of the boat and started running all around. It was fun, but very surprising, to watch which we did until she, and we, fell asleep.

The sun came up hours ago. It was so stunning because the two moons were still above the horizon and their silhouettes were on either side of the sun, but that didn't stop the waterfall at Warrego Valles from glowing like a stream of cascading diamonds as the sun hit the falling water. The water itself was falling down the face of a mountain that had to have been taller than the biggest skyscraper they ever built on Earth.

"Pandorica wake up and take a look," I said as I took her hand. She was still tired and a little grumpy when she asked me what I wanted. "Look...there it is! There's Warrego Valles." The minute she heard that she jumped to her feet and her face was covered with the biggest smile I had ever seen. "We made it...we made it!"

We grabbed up Rhosly and started out across the plains to the base of the waterfall. It was dry and hot, but for some reason it didn't matter. We were too happy to feel any discomfort. Even the baby was laughing and playing as we walked. Then we saw it. There was a line of poles going off in either direction and each pole had a warning that read, "Do not proceed. You cannot survive going any farther."

"What does that mean?" Pandorica asked. "This has always been a site of peace and renewal. I do not understand."

I went up to one of the poles. The warning posted there looked old... very old. Immediately I decided that Pandorica and Rhosly should stay behind, and that I would proceed alone. Of course that started one hell of an argument between Pandorica and I, she was so concerned, but eventually I put an end to it and it was agreed, for Rhosly's sake, I would investigate the area before they came with me. But, before I left, I made sure that the two of them were going to be safe. I set about building a small shelter on the edge of the river. I also filled some containers with water and even caught them some fish so they would not be hungry and then it was time to go, so I kissed them goodbye, grabbed the white sword and started out alone.

As I walked the air got heavier and heavier. It was full of sulfur. I mean it was so strong that I could hardly breathe so I slowed way down and took deep breaths as often as I could. That helped some, but not that much. It felt like I was walking through the inner rings of hell. The sword hung by my side. It was getting even hotter than the air was. It got so bad that I could feel the skin on the outside of my leg start to burn. It wasn't serious but I could still feel it through my pants.

The waterfall was still about a mile from me. Looking back, I could no longer see Pandorica, I was truly alone. *If I die how long would it take Pandorica to realize it*, I thought. I didn't want to have thoughts like that, but I couldn't help it. The air was so nice back with them, and so like the fires of hell here. How could I make it back out?

That last mile was so hard, I ended up crawling for the last quarter of a mile. My hands and knees were covered with blood when I finally reached the waterfall. My eyes were burning with what sweat, I had left, which wasn't much. I was dying but then something happened. When I completed my mission and put the blade of the sword into the waterfall, the air around me cooled to where I could breathe once again.

The blade was glowing with a very bright light, so our mission had been accomplished, yet though I wanted to be with Pandorica and Rhosly as fast as I could, I was just too exhausted to make the return trip at that moment. So, I decided that I would take a short nap before I started back… maybe just a couple of hours. That would allow my body to return to normal and allow me to find my way quickly back to area to where I had left them. But, before I did I, needed to rest.

# ENTRY 51
## 26.04.63.21.35

I slept a little longer than I thought I was going to. The air was still cool and that was nice. The sun was just above the horizon when I woke up and started walking back. It wasn't going to be a long trip, and luckily the heat I had endured earlier, when I actually thought I would not survive had miraculously passed. Thank God that was over!

Before I left I filled a small container with some of the water from the falls. It was so cold that ice immediately formed all over the glass.

I walked as quickly as my strength would allow me, and had walked about a half an hour, and yeah, I was tired, but I had to keep going, as all I wanted to do now was get back to Pandorica and Rhosly. But then I saw something I really never wanted or expected to see. In the dust of the desert I saw two bodies lying next to each other. I could see them breathing, but they were not moving. I walked over and gently rolled the two bodies over. As I did I let out a horrified cry. The bodies were Pandorica and Rhosly. They had foolishly started following me in that heat, and Pandorica had not thought to bring enough water so they dropped where they had stood.

Their breathing was shallow... so shallow that although their chests were moving I could not hear them taking in any air. The baby's skin was starting to turn blue as I grabbed her up and held her close to me. "What can I do," I yelled to the heavens. "I am not going to lose them now." Rhosly's eyes began to glaze over and I swear that I saw her lips form the word daddy. Her skin was burning hot despite the air temperature so I took the water container from my pocket and gave her a sip. Her eyes flickered a bit and then opened wide.

"Daddy," she said in a crisp, clear voice. Then she called for her mommy. I let her rest as I ran over to Pandorica. She was much worse off than Rhosly had been. Her skin was dried out and starting to peel. Her eyes were closed and I could not feel a heartbeat. "Daddy, what's wrong with mommy," she asked. Her voice was cracking and I could see tears running down her face.

"She's going to be alright," I said. I couldn't be sure, as a matter of fact, I had my doubts.

Her eyelids flickered a bit as if she was still there somewhere deep inside. I raised her head from the sand. Some of her scales had fallen into the dirt and I saw traces of blood coming from some small open wounds. "Pandorica," I whispered. "If you can hear me please don't leave me." I took the water container, placed it on her lips and let a couple drops fall in. Then I took the rest of the water and rubbed it all over her body. Nothing happened! "PANDORICA," I cried out just before I kissed her on the forehead. "I WANT YOU BACK AND I WANT

YOU BACK NOW. I LOVE YOU TOO MUCH TO LOSE YOU!"

"I love you too," she said in a weak voice as her eyes opened.

I didn't waste a second. I scooped them both up in my arms and carried them both the mile and a half back to camp. There I sat them in the water to cool them off. I gathered some fish to feed them and then I put them to bed for the night. Me, I am just going to sit and look at that goddamn sword. *Was it all worth it*, I thought. I wasn't going to know that until I got back, but I seriously doubted it.

ENTRY 52
28.04.63.15.12


It has been two days and Pandorica and Rhosly were coming in and out of consciousness again and again. I am so worried about them. There were some dead trees nearby so I managed, with a lot of effort, to build a semi-decent shelter. It wasn't much, but it was enough to keep the night's winds and the burning sun off of them.

There was something wrong and I had no idea what it was. It was almost as if something had just come in a taken their life force away from them and just left enough for them to stay alive. Then a flash once again came to me and I remembered something like that from horror films back on earth. Vampires would attack someone and drink enough blood to quench their thirsts and leave enough blood to keep the person alive so they could feed again later. There was one movie where a vampire fed from the same person four or five times before they let them die.

I did my best to feed them both and give them water but they weren't getting any better. They were actually a lot worse!

Something was coming up on the camp. I could hear them on the other side of a big rock on the north side of the clearing. Grabbing a stick from the side of the river I stood up, braced myself and waited for whatever it was to come around. It didn't take long. I don't remember if I smiled or what when I first saw them. It was two soldiers from Tergina.

"Williams from Phoenix...," one of them said. "... What has happened here?" I explained to them what had happened, and I showed them the sword, but they weren't interested in that they wanted to care for Pandorica and Rhosly. "We do not have room for you, but we will take Gavabu and the little princess back to our village and we will give them the best treatment we can." They both dismounted, picked the two of them up, remounted their creatures and started to leave, but before they rode off, one of them said, "I have seen this before Williams from Phoenix and it grieves me so to tell you, but there is very little hope that they will survive." Then they rode off.

I didn't know what to do other them, follow them as best as I could. Crying, that would come later. Right now, I had to get to that village to take care of my wife and baby and that is all.

ENTRY 53
29.04.63.14.03


I decided that it would be better if I stayed on the top of the canyon rather than travel along the river below. It was easier to travel and would cut a few hours off of my journey... that was, until I found this woman wandering through some rocks.

"Who are you?" I asked as she stepped from the rocks and walked over to me. Yeah, I was surprised to see another Human this far away from the Human cities, but I was also happy to see a Human anywhere on this planet.

"My name is Erinna," she said with a smile on her face and what a beautiful face it was. She had freckles on ivory white skin, red hair and aquamarine eyes. "I have been sent here looking for a man who visited my city some time ago." When she described her city I knew that I was that man, and when I told her, she said that something terrible had happened, and her people had to evacuate the city. "We are hoping that you can help us!"

*Why does everyone on this planet think I can help them*, I thought. I didn't tell her, yes or no, but I did tell her that I had something important to take care of, and that I would find her as soon as I could and that I would try to help..

She didn't say a word, but her eyes showed disappointment and even anger. I was obviously distracted, and so I was truly shocked when suddenly she jumped at me. In one movement she knocked me to the ground and took the white sword from the sheath. "When you decide what is important, then this will be returned to you," she growled as she broke into a run back into the rocks.

"I need that," I yelled, but to no avail, she was gone. I tried to follow her for a while, but the going was too hard and she was too fast, so I turned back on course and once again started walking back to Tergina.

## ENTRY 54
## 30.04.63.11.27

I walked until it got too dark to go any further, then I found a shrub and settled down for the night. My mind was going wild, so even when I did start resting, I could not sleep. I kept thinking about Pandorica and Rhosly. Were they still alive? Did they make it back to the village? Were they going to be alright? But, even though my thoughts were on them, my mind would not let me forget that woman, Erinna, her anger, and why she stopped me and then stole the sword.

What in the hell did she want me to do? Yeah, I did remember the city and I didn't really like it there. I would rather help the Zartoon than the Humans on this planet. I also knew one thing, I needed that sword back, but for the present that had to wait. My family needed me and I was going to get back to them no matter what.

The way I figure, I should make it by nightfall if I keep walking, so that is what I'm going to do. The rest can wait until tomorrow.

ENTRY 55
02.05.63.17.00


I finally made it back to Tergina. I am bruised and bloodied, but my spirits are still strong, and it was made even stronger when I got to the gates and I was met by the village's leader.

"You have come to see Gavabu and her child," he asked.

"She is my wife and the child is my daughter," I replied. I don't know how but I got the courage up to make a demand. "I would like to see them and see them now." My voice was strange, even for me but it got the message through. He escorted me to a room where a young adult was resting on a small but fancy bed.

The woman turned to me and all she could say was, "Daddy!" Then she got up and ran across the room and into my arms.

"Rhosly," I asked in bewilderment as I took her hand. "Is it really you?" She looked at me and smiled and replied that yes, she was my daughter. "What happened to you? I inquired, "when I saw you last you were a child, and so close to death when they took you away from me and brought you and your mother back to Tergina."

"Yes, father when they brought us here as you know we were both very seriously ill and close to death," she said. "So here they gave me some kind of herbs, and then within a few passing moments I was feeling better and up on my feet again." She then explained, that due to her youth, and the rapid growth a Zartoon human child goes through, it increased her metabolism to such a high rate that the herbs were able to work almost immediately.

"What about your mother?" I asked. I didn't want to know... not really... especially if it was bad news, but I had to ask.

"Unfortunately, my mother's metabolism isn't as good as mine," Rhosly cried as a tear started rolling down her cheek. "They gave her the same herbs they gave me, but they just didn't work as they did on me. She is still close to death, they even have priestesses praying over her, burning ancient bundles of secret herbs, and they also sent a messenger to get water from the falls where we were stricken. They have not returned yet."

I couldn't take anymore. Rhosly didn't have any more to tell me, so I found out where Pandorica was, and I rushed over to where they were attending to her. The door was blocked by a guard who had to have been the biggest, ugliest and meanest Zartoon I had ever seen. I politely asked to enter the room. "No one... especially a Human... is allowed in the room until the Princess is ready!" I explained who I was and he still would not allow me to enter. Finally, one of the priestesses walked from the room and I could see through a crack when she opened the door. I saw Pandorica lying on some kind of bed. It was huge and covered with a deep purple and black comforter. All around her were priestesses wearing black cloaks. They were stroking her face with damp cloths, placing water on her lips and praying at her feet, but from what I could see, my Pandorica was not moving. I could not even see her chest move as she breathed. Still, at least these Zartoon were not giving up. Unfortunately, I was not able to see or hear any more before I was chased away and told that under no uncertain terms was I to go back to that room.

I went back to Rhosly and we sat and talked, I was trying my best to believe Pandorica would survive, and my dear grown up little Rhosly was trying her best to comfort me. We then went to eat some God-forsaken Zartoon food, and I decided to then head back to the rooms they had provided for us and to try to get some sleep. I needed to think calmly and clearly so I could find a way to see my wife and get passed the formidable Zartoon guard at her door.

## ENTRY 56
## 03.05.63.09.58

I thought of something last night. I, at first, thought I would run it by the village elders, but then I thought, maybe not, talking to them might be a waste of time... time that Pandorica doesn't have.

I did mention what I was planning to Rhosly and she thought that it was a good idea... not great but still a good idea. It meant that I had to leave the village. That was something I really didn't want to do, but I didn't want to lose Pandorica either.

The first thing I did once I made up my mind was that Rhosly and I were going to see her mother. Once we got there, I argued so loud and fought like hell, until eventually the guard finally weakened, even so he stubbornly kept on refusing, but finally, we talked him into letting us visit and we walked into the room.

Pandorica was still lying on the bed where I had seen her the day before. She was hooked up to monitors, restraints and more than a dozen tubes and bags. I could see her eyes fluttering and the corners of her mouth twitched ever so slightly so she was still in there. Then I saw what I could only call a miracle...when I spoke to her I saw the scales above her eyes move as if she was trying to respond to my voice.

"Rhosly," I said. "You stay here with your

mother. I have someone I have to find. I don't know where she is, but I swear to you that I will find her, and I will come back to you, and I will bring your mother back." She didn't say a word as I leaned over and kissed Pandorica with all of the love I had in my heart. Then I kissed Rhosly and I walked out of the room and then out of the village.

No one tried to stop me and God help them if they had. I was on a mission to save my wife and not any man, Zartoon, human or anything else was going to stop me.

ENTRY 57
05.05.63.16.58


I finally made it back to where that woman, Erinna, talked to me. You know, sometimes the weather just cooperates with you. There had obviously been no wind to speak of, because her footprints were as clear as the moment she walked away. I guess I should thank the gods for that, but after what they did to Pandorica, I really don't want to talk, either to them or even to the God I grew up with. I still don't understand why he, or they, did what they did, but I can't really think about that now, I have to find that sword.

Erinna had headed off into the desert, and she already had a couple of days head start. It was going to be hard and a long trip, so I psyched myself up and started out at 08.20. Let's see, that was eight hours ago. I am tired and thirsty. I didn't bring enough water with me, but I do know how to survive... not thrive but just survive. I would do what they did on Earth, especially in the Sahara or the Painted Desert. I would drink water from the plants on my way. There weren't very many, but there were enough.

"Fa Nex, you must keep going no matter what," a voice said in my mind. "I am waiting for you. I am not going to leave you. I love you too much." I listened carefully to the voice.

It sounded a little like Pandorica, but it was somehow different. It was softer, more distant than I had heard before. "I know who you are looking for. She is not far ahead of you... maybe a day. I know that you can make it." Then the voice just went silent, but even in its silence, I was motivated. I was determined to catch that woman, get the sword back and save my Pandorica.

I am not going to stop to sleep tonight. The moons will be bright enough for me to see where I am going. I want to be within hours of her when the sun comes up. I don't know, rather let me say I am not sure, what I am going to do, but one way or the other I am going to be holding that sword by sunset tomorrow. I promise myself that!

ENTRY 58
06.05.63.10.58


I walked all night long. I think it was about four in the morning when I saw the glow of a fire coming from over a hill about five miles away. I thought I had found Erinna. I made it to the hill a couple hours later. The sun was coming up, but the sky was cloudy, so the air was cool and it was actually relaxing. That was something I was counting on. I was hoping that, maybe, if this was the camp, she would sleep in, since Erinna probably felt secure that I wasn't going to find her. How wrong could she be?

I walked slow down the hill. It was nothing but sand and a few sparse blades of grass so I had a hard time keeping my balance and, if I fell, I might make some noise that would alert Erinna that I was coming.

The tent flap was open. What nerve, or stupidity, my enemy had, and she was that, as she has stolen the white sword. I didn't walk in, instead I went down on my hands and knees, crawling as slowly and quietly as I could until I got right inside the tent and up next to her.

"Erinna," I yelled as I jumped on top of her, wrapping my hands tightly around her throat. Her arms were pinned beneath my knees, so she couldn't move and my hands made sure that she couldn't breathe either. "You move, and I swear to the gods that I will break your neck!" I stated, terrifying her as much as I could. I knew that she had to be taking me very seriously, because she was turning blue and her eyes were rolling back into her skull before I allowed her to take a breath.

"What do you want?" Erinna asked as soon as she got her breath back.

I told her that I wanted the sword back, but before she could answer I saw the sword hiding under her bedroll. I bent down to grab it, and the second I did, she managed to roll over and, with unbelievable strength, to throw me to the ground. Then she leapt from the bed and started choking me. I was, literally, choking to death, and I knew Erinna was certainly about to kill me. Deep inside, I sure did not want to do what I had to do, but I also knew this was the only way I could save myself and my Pandorica. So with Herculean strength I did what I had to do. I quickly brought the sword up and shoved the blade through the side of Erinna's throat.

"I told you," was all I could say as the limp body fell to the ground twitching in the throes of death. Killing anyone, especially a woman is not something I ever thought I could do, but like I said, I really didn't want to do it, but I did... she had to die.

I didn't stop to bury her just in case she had friends who would show up at any moment, so I just grabbed the sword and started the walk back to Tergina.

## ENTRY 59
## 08.05.63.17.00

I was just a few miles from Tergina when I woke up this morning. There hasn't been much time for me to think up until now. I have no idea how the white sword is going to help Pandorica, but something tells me that it will, and that I will know how to use it once I get there.

The thoughts about that girl still haunt me. What in the hell did she need me for? Why were the Humans in such trouble? Maybe it was the same thing that affected the Zartoon city. I had no idea, but that was behind me, so I had to put the thoughts behind me and just think about Pandorica and Rhosly and what I could do for them.

Finally, I was at the gates of Tergina. The guards didn't even try to stop me... not that they could if they had tried. Instead, they escorted me through the village and right up to the room where Pandorica was sleeping.

Her breathing was severely labored and, although her eyes were open, they were glazed over, and I doubt that she could see anything. I watched as her body twitched and her hands tightened and loosened as if she was trying to grab something. I took her hand in mine and gently squeezed it. I could feel her pulse though her fingers. It was weak... very weak... but it was there.

"Her Highness may not make it," a priest said from behind me. Then he instructed me to come with him. He talked to me in a voice that wasn't even a whisper.

"I will not do that," I said in an angry voice as I shoved him and stepped back against a rock. "How could you even suggest that I do that to her?" My anger didn't dissipate as he explained that I was the only person who could save Pandorica's life and I had to do it right then, or it would be too late. I started crying, but reluctantly agreed.

He dressed me in a white robe and blessed me with the smoke from some herb that he said had been passed down for thousands of years. It smelled good…maybe too good. It made me think of the pot I smoked as a kid. "This will help you relax and do what you must do." Then he walked me back to Pandorica. I stood beside her as he and a group of other Zartoon walked in, surrounded her and started chanting.

I climbed upon the bed where Pandorica was lying. The priest handed me the white sword I had been carrying, I raised it above my head just as he had told me to do. I looked and the blade was glowing with a bright white light. I guess he saw that I didn't want to do what he told me to do, because his hand reached out and touched me on the thigh. "You have to," he said in a soothing voice.

I gripped the sword tightly. I could feel its power flowing into me. Suddenly, I took the blade and drove it into Pandorica's chest. As the blade entered her body her eyes opened and she looked at me with eyes that were full of pain and fear. Her body tightened beneath me and I felt her go into one convulsion after another. Her blood flowed onto the bed and then on the ground.

My body and mind went into shock. Then last thing I remember was looking into her face, I could not stand to see what she was going through. My body must have agreed, because in just a few seconds, I felt myself fading into darkness and I felt as I began to fall off of the bed. Then, I was out!

ENTRY 60
10.05.63.11.53

I woke up about an hour ago. I feel so bad. I should have been there taking care of Pandorica. Maybe I killed her... I don't know if I did or not. There was so much blood all over the room. How could she have lived through that? Nobody has told me anything and I am not allowed out of bed.

It took this long for my eyes to focus and, once again, get used to the light. The first person I saw was Rhosly. She was standing silently, looking at me and beside her was a young man. I had a feeling that I had seen him before somewhere. Yeah, he had some of the scales of a Zartoon but he had such strong Human features including a flesh colored skin and blonde hair down to his shoulders. "Who are you," I asked the man as Rhosly walked over and sat on the edge of my bed.

"Fa Nex, I am your son, Bledri," he replied. His smile was mixed with happiness and concern but he was smiling.

"How... why are you here," I asked.

"Someone from Tergina came to my village and summoned me," he said. "They said that my mother was ill and I was needed immediately." The slits in his eyes closed as I saw a tear run down his cheek. "I got here just in time." I started crying into my hands as I watched Bledri's tear hit the ground. He must have realized what I was thinking because he immediately added to what he had said. "Fa Nex," he started. "I got here just as they were carrying you out, and Pandorica was waking up just as I stepped through the door. She knew me right off as her son."

"Then Pandorica is...," I started.

"Alive," Bledri said. "Yes, she is alive and she shows no effects from either the disease or the cure... not even a scar."

I was most thankfully happy to hear that. I was so afraid that I had killed my beloved Pandorica. Then a question ran through my head that I just had to ask before anything else happened. "How did the Terginas know about you?" I asked.

"There must be a Human/Zartoon hybrid in the village," a female voice said from the door. I looked, and there was my Pandorica, walking into the room with a number of other Zartoon following her. I sat up on the edge of the bed, nearly knocking Rhosly to the floor. Pandorica immediately ran over and hugged me before she continued. "Although neither Humans, nor Zartoon are telepathic, if you combine our DNA, the child can read the mind of anyone they desire. I guess I was thinking about our son, so they sent someone to retrieve him."

The four of us sat in that room until far after sunset just talking and getting to know each other. I loved that, but I also knew that I had something I had to do. I have something that I have to write in this diary that I do not, ever want them to see, so I will be back after they are sleeping to finish this.

ENTRY 61
11.05.63.02.53


While I was out I had a vision that I have
to keep to myself. If I told anyone, the Zartoon
would lock me up as a lunatic. But I cannot just
keep this in my head. I have to write it down so
that, if it happens, there will be a record of what
happened.

I saw Zartoon. It was about a hundred years
from now. There was a major war between the
Humans and the Zartoon. It went on for years
and years and the ground was covered with
bodies and blood flowed, where the life giving
water once filled the rivers. I am not sure, but
I think that the only cities left were the ones I
visited earlier. They had very few living there,
that is if you can call the walking dead living.

I saw Pandorica's great-great-great
grandson. He was leading an army of about
four hundred Zartoon and hybrids. Most of
them were wounded, but not bad enough to
stop them from defending their city.

The Humans also still lived in their Human
city. I have no idea how many of them were left,
but I had a strong feeling that their numbers
were about the same as the Zartoon. One thing
I remember seeing was two Zartoon talking as
they ate their afternoon meal. "My grandfather
told me that all of this started when that Human
from Yartook got back with the sword. It was

supposed to protect us, but the power it was supposed to carry was gone. He was selfish and used it to save his wife. Yes, it saved her alright, but the white sword meant to save us all, it had lost all its power when he handed it over to the Zartoon Council. So the Humans took that as a sign that Zartoon could be theirs, and they took advantage of it, and the blood soon flowed."

I waited to hear the rest, but as soon as he finished that sentence, a missile came flying above the city. There was a big flash of light, the hottest heat I had ever felt and a wind that destroyed everything it hit. After everything was done, there was nothing... no buildings, no bodies... nothing!

*Those bastards brought it with them*, I thought. *They destroyed Earth and now they are doing the same thing to Zartoon.* I could feel myself starting to cry. I do not know if it was sadness or anger, but I was crying.

In my vision I did not see the Human city, but, if it survived the winds, they were downwind, so I am sure that the radiation would have killed every damn one of them. It would have taken longer, maybe years, but they were going to die eventually, and that pleased me no end.

I have a feeling that that vision was accurate, I now remember how we humans were on the Earth, we fought and killed over money, land... hell, we even fought over fighting and now in my vision I can see it is going to happen here all

over again… but this time I can do something…
I can stop it… I just can't tell anyone why I am
going to do, what I have to do.

I have been quiet about what I saw in my vision. I haven't even told Pandorica about it.

There was one thing I noticed this morning... the white sword wasn't glowing any longer. I can only guess that it lost its radiation when I used it to save Pandorica, but I believe that it was still worth it. Pandorica's life over the Zartoon village... that was a no brainer. Of course I would save her! It was then that Bledri walked over to me.

"Father, do not worry," he said in a calming voice.

"What do you mean," I asked.

"The power of the water is still within the sword," he said. "It had been shared with mother, but there are still remnants enough for you to do what must be done." I didn't ask him how he knew what I was thinking. Then I suddenly remember that he was telepathic. "Rhosly and I will stay with you to help you and protect you. It is vital to the Zartoon race that you make it safely." Then he asked me about my vision.

I told him everything about it. Hell, he knew everything anyway so I figured I might as well. Then, after I spilled everything, I had a thought... if he could read my mind... I wondered if Rhosly could read it too? I looked over and Rhosly was talking to her mother. I couldn't tell what they were talking about and to be honest, I didn't want to.

After about an hour of talking I thought that it was a good time to start back to the Zartoon village... if they were still where we left them, that is. Bledri and Rhosly left about ten minutes before Pandorica and I. I didn't mind! I was happy to have her alone with me so we could talk as a couple with no one else around. I guess that's the wish of every set of parents, and I had to travel to Zartoon to find it!

ENTRY 63
15.05.63.21.45


We have been walking for three days now. You have no idea how much I wished that I hadn't lost that traveler, I had a month ago. It would be so great to just zip across the sand and get back to the village. The way I figure, we have done a little over one hundred miles, and we still had miles to go. It is so far and so desolate, but we have to make it.

Bledri was ahead of us, with the Rhosly right by his side. I am kind of nervous about it. Considering they didn't even know each other a few days ago, they have become a little too close for my liking. I swear when they left Pandorica and I this morning, they were actually holding hands, and they were looking into each other's eyes, the way Pandorica and I look at each other.

"Pandorica," I called. As soon as she walked over to me, I asked her what was going on with the kids. I told her that it was making me uncomfortable.

"Fa Nex, they are young and you worry too much," she said with a big smile and a flick of her tongue. I didn't exactly what that meant, but it kept my attention locked on her. "You know the way some young animals practice war and attacking their prey. Well, they are young and just also playing getting to know each other. Remember Fa Nex you told me even Human children on Earth play strange games, like what do you call it, Cowboys and? ..."

"It is just play," I said. "Games to teach Human children what life could be like and prepare them for it. Human life is a lot harder than anything the Zartoon could ever imagine/"

"I do not know about that," Pandorica said with a bite in her voice and a grimace across her face. "We certainly do not teach our children the art of war! But it is there, it is always there, it must, I suppose it comes from our ancient DNA. For so many years, ever since I can remember, most Zartoon and Humans have been enemies and many have died. Because of this, the Zartoon council years ago, decided to teach our children about life, instead of war and violence.

Fa Nex, please do not worry about Rhosly and Bledri, in Zartoon young teenagers so often "hook up" with someone who they know and trust. I have only seen it twice where the two siblings went too far... Yes, they married and mated, but luckily no children were born. Believe me it happens so rarely, that the sacred learning of the ways has been broken.

"How do we..." I started to ask.

"We don't... we can't," Pandorica said. "Trust me... if Rhosly feels that Bledri is going too far and turning it into a problem... she will take care of it in her own way."

Thinking over what Pandorica said, I realized that I had not seen the two of them less than three feet apart since they met and exchanged a hug, so I guess that she was right and all the kids were doing was "practicing" the same mating rituals that every young being in the universe must practice,

Anyway, forgetting all of that, Bledri suddenly came back to me and Pandorica and said that he found something about five miles ahead. We only took about a hour to make it that far... thank the gods for Zartoon gravity!

When we got there, it was a wall... made out of sandstone and it stretched out for miles in either direction. Looking at it kind of reminded me of Hadrian's Wall in northern England. "That wasn't here when we came this way earlier," I said as I just stared ahead.

"I didn't see it either," Bledri said.

"They couldn't have built anything like that so quick," I said to Pandorica. Then she did something completely logical, but I didn't expect it. She picked up a rock a gave it a hard throw right at the base of the wall. It didn't bounce off it didn't even make a sound when it hit the wall. The rock just disappeared!

Rhosly, who had been watching the wall since they found it, walked up to the wall and touched it, but there was nothing there! Her hand went right into the wall, and when she pulled it out, she was fine. Then, as any daughter of mine would do, she took the next step and walked into the wall. It was a couple of minutes before she returned, but she was laughing and having a good time when she did.

"I can't believe it," she said. "I honestly can't believe it! I walked through it and you can't see it from the other side. It just isn't there! Well. It is there, but it isn't there. That's why we didn't see it before... we never looked back!"

I was the next to go through followed by Bledri, Pandorica, and lastly Rhosly. Then, of course we all walked back through, and then back again. It was really strange. I could tell why Rhosly was so happy when she stepped back through. There was a sense of pure euphoria when you walked through. It wasn't a high like you'd get from drugs or alcohol... it was just a feeling of utter peace and happiness.

I could imagine what the purpose of the wall was... to stop anyone from heading into that territory from the north, but still let "people" go the other way, but I couldn't imagine what technology would be powerful to maintain an illusion like that. It must be massive. I would love to check it out if I ever come back, but right now... we had something to do and someplace to be so we just kept walking.

## ENTRY 64
## 17.05.63.13.22

Bledri left last night. He wanted to go further ahead to see what was going on ahead of us. That wasn't unusual… he left every night, but he was always there when we woke up it the morning, but this morning he wasn't there.

The rising sun showed a faint set of footprints leading off toward the Zartoon village, but there were no other signs that he had even been with us. Then I noticed that Rhosly wasn't anywhere to be seen. Pandorica must have noticed the same thing because she started yelling out for the kids, but there was no answer. "They must have gone too far, and couldn't make it back," she said.

"That has to be it," I said as I started packing things up. "I think we should follow those tracks and see where they went." She agreed so we started out.

It wasn't long before we heard a strange noise coming from in front of us. It took us another minute or two, but when we found the noise, we saw Rhosly laying on the sand. The noise was her crying, in fact, she was bawling her eyes out. We ran over and Pandorica lifted her up and cradled her head in her arms. Rhosly looked up at her. "There was nothing I could do," she said between her sob. "We were so far away and it was so dark. There was nothing I could do. I swear mother… there was nothing I could do."

"What do you mean?" I asked. Rhosly didn't answer, she just took her mother by the hand and started walking into the desert. "Rhosly, where are we going?" I asked as I took her other hand. Still, she didn't say a word, she just kept walking.

It was about another five miles before Rhosly fell to her knees. She was crying so hard her body was convulsing. "There," she said… nothing else just "there".

Pandorica stayed with her, as I went over to see what had her so upset. There was a body lying in the sand, it was badly burnt, and was hardly recognizable, but the way Rhosly was acting it wasn't hard to figure out who it was.

I ran back and looked into Rhosly's eyes. They were full of pain so that confirmed to me who it was.

"What happened?" I asked as I held my own tears back.

"We were resting before coming back and a group of Humans came out of the forest," she said. "Bledri heard them coming, and he hid me in the sand. They came and just beat him to death, and then they set fire to his body. They wanted a female, but he protected me, though they kept beating him, he would not tell them where I was. He gave his life to save me." Then she broke down and asked Pandorica, why these Humans would do such a thing.

She didn't answer, what could she say to soothe Rhosly. There was nothing that would make it any better

I sat on a nearby rock and just thought. It was my fault for letting him go ahead and not making him stay with us. That made me think that maybe I should use the sword on myself, so he would not be alone, but I thought about Rhosly and Pandorica, and I could not leave them out here all by themselves. I had to keep my mind straight and not mourn... not right now. There would be time for that later.

Anyway, I dug a shallow grave with my hands and laid my son into the opening, while Pandorica and Rhosly prayed to their gods and I prayed to mine. Then Pandorica and Rhosly kissed him on the cheek and I covered his body.

We all said our last goodbyes and started out again. It was not safe there. Those men might come back and we had no way to defend ourselves. Besides that I was NOT going to let my son die in vain. The sword wouldn't save anyone, unless we got it back to the Zartoon Council, so we left the unmarked grave and continued back to the Zartoon camp. It is with deep, overwhelming sadness that I write this entry.

ENTRY 65
17.05.63.19.51


    I wish I would have more time to get to know Bledri, and I sure wish we would have had more time to mourn him, but that wasn't possible. There will be time for that later... once we get back to Pandorica's people.

    While we were walking, I started talking to Pandorica. I was told that the Humans and the Zartoon began coexisting in peace, and I wanted to know why things changed so drastically.

    "Before the Humans arrived, Zartoon was green and alive," Pandorica said as Rhosly came back and listened to her. "When they came, the water dried up, and most of the plants and animals died off. It wasn't long before the Humans would come to our villages, settlements, and cities and steal food and water, and take some of the younger ones as slaves. We became not even second-class citizens on our own planet. We became animals to the Humans. We knew how to live jn our world, and how to survive on it, and they didn't, and they hated us for it. Now, it is not all of them, and as you see we have accepted the ones who are friends and they are welcomed into our cities. They still want to live in peace, but there were enough who wanted only war, to survive we have to defend ourselves."

    "I have a question," I said. I was surprised

I hadn't asked before, but it never crossed my mind until just then. "What will the white sword do when we give it back?"

She didn't answer… as a matter of fact, she quickly changed the subject and pointed to one of the Human satellites that the United States had launched for exploration. "Darling Fa Nex, when I was little I used to spend so many nights looking up and watching those stars as they moved across the sky," she said. "I was taught that if you see one you are supposed to make a wish. I have so many wishes that I am waiting for that star to answer. Maybe someday… don't you think?" I watched as Pandorica and Rhosly stared into the sky and they each made a wish.

The sun is down now, as you could probably tell from what I wrote. Anyway, I climbed on top of a nearby hill and I could see the glow of campfires coming for a couple of hour travel from here, but it is too late now and we have had a really bad day so we are just going to camp here for the night and get to the Zartoon camp in the morning.

ENTRY 66
18.05.63.11.20


We woke up about an hour ago. Pandorica suggested that it would be better if she walked into the village first, and then for Rhosly and I to follow a little later, after she had the chance to talk to the Zartoon leaders.

She was gone for a couple of hours, and the entire time she was gone, we could hear an uproar coming from everyone in the camp. It wasn't a bad uproar... it was more of cheering and celebration. I guess they were happy to know that the white sword was so close. Now, it was our turn to go in.

Rhosly walked in beside me, and we were met like we were gods or something. I was actually placed on some Zartoon's shoulders and carried through the streets and right up to the place where the Council was waiting. "Welcome back Fa Nex," one of the elders said. "We mourn you loss, but we are also so happy that you, Pandorica, and Rhosly have returned safely." Then he looked into my eyes and told me that a squad of Zartoon warriors would be sent out immediately to find and punish those responsible for Bledri's death.

I thanked him and told him where the men were and then I took the sword from my pouch and handed it to the Council. The sword was glowing brighter than it had before. It was almost as if it had a mind and it knew what was happening. Suddenly, the sword started vibrating and it created one of the strangest sounds I had ever heard. The thing was, the more distance between the sword and me... the louder the sound got.

"Fa Nex," the elder said. I knew what he was going to say so I walked over to him and held my hand out. He placed the sword in my hand and it went strangely silent. "This is amazing! The white sword has chosen you... a non Zartoon. That has never happened before. You are the one who has to see this through to the end."

I had no idea what that meant. The way I saw it, I had done everything I had been asked... even more, and now they wanted me to do more. I was really too tired to argue that I didn't want to do anymore and, besides that, Pandorica broke in that we would be honored to help out again.

We weren't going to have a lot of time before we had to leave once again, all we had time to do was spend some time with Rhosly, pack our things and get ready to leave. We also spent time getting instructions. We weren't told what the sword would do, and just where we had to go and what we had to do. So, we will be leaving very soon, but for now it is time to rest, eat and also think a whole hell of a lot.

ENTRY 67
19.05.63.19.56

We left this morning. All I could think of was, why, I had to be the one. This is not even my world. I shouldn't be here! For some reason this white sword, has picked me and Pandorica to finish this "mission." I am honestly very tired of it! Maybe I should have stayed with the Humans when I had the chance, but that may not have been a good thing either. I have never been so torn.

On the way we saw some Human patrols. It was just a few, but they were still there. I'm glad they didn't see us otherwise they would have come over to question us, and most likely Pandorica would have been taken by them, or at the worse they would have executed her on the spot. I didn't want to risk any of that happening. I guess from now on, I'll have to be a lot more observant if we want to stay alive and complete our mission .

"How did they get so close to the village?" Pandorica asked. "They should have been intercepted the second they got within a couple of hours of the village." I had no idea what to say… maybe the Zartoon had become too sure that they were hiding well. Well, if you ask me… they weren't.

Well, that was hours ago. Now, the sun is going down and amazingly both of the moons were new moons, so outside of the light of the stars, it was nearly black when we finally saw sight of the Zartoon city. I could see travelers zipping across the sand and small ships buzzing through between the buildings. It almost looked as if the Zartoon had never left, but there were some big differences. The first I noticed were large pulse cannons on the walls of the city. I know for a fact that they were not there before.

Now, I wasn't scared for me... not in the least. I could fit in, but I was terrified for Pandorica. I had no idea how the Humans were treating the Zartoon any longer and I sure didn't want to find out by risking her life.

In the morning I will make sure that she is well hidden and I'll go into the city and do whatever it is I'm supposed to do and get my ass out of there, but until then I am just going to hold Pandorica in my arms and try and get some sleep.

ENTRY 68
20.05.63.12.01

I woke up before the sun came up this morning. It was still dark as hell, but I could see a glow of light coming from behind the city. I could not believe what I was seeing. For it being so freaking early and so cold, yet the former Zartoon city was as busy as I now remember New York City being, which I suddenly now remember I visited when I was a kid. As soon as we had eaten, I sent Pandorica into a forest I had seen the night before. It was about a mile away from where we camped, so she could safely hide there until I got back.

It took me about an hour before I got to the city gates. They were heavily guarded, but they didn't stop me when I walked through. That was one major problem avoided. There were men, women, and children running through the streets, playing games and running the shops where Zartoon used to run their businesses.

*They look so happy… so normal*, I thought. Of course, kids being kids, the second some of the children saw me they ran up and started asking me for candy or some of the small gemstones they used for money. I didn't have either, so I just brushed them away and continued my way through the streets. Finally an older man came up to me and shook my hand.

"You are new to our city my friend," he said

with a smile. "Please, if there is anything you need just let me know. We do so love it when we get visitors." I heard what he said, but I really wasn't paying that much attention to him. The sword in my bag was heating up and it was becoming so warm that I could feel it through the bag and the many layers of clothes I was wearing.

"I heard that this city used to belong to the creatures of this planet," I asked.

"Yes, this was a Zartoon city," he replied. "They deserted it many, many centuries ago and we colonized it for Human life." Now, I knew better, but I thought it would be better if I didn't say anything. "I think the ones who used to live here must have died off or something," he said.

"Are there any of the old buildings left?" I asked. He pointed at a couple of the buildings that really didn't interest me but then he pointed out a temple at the center of the city. That was what I was looking for! I didn't say another word. I just turned and started walking to the temple with the old man following right behind me.

I was nearly to the door when I noticed something. There were only a few Zartoon walking around the street and they were NOT walking the way I had seen them before. Most of them were carrying extreme weights. Some of them were attached to harnesses and were dragging loads that no Human could ever drag.

They had gone from being servants and mates to beasts of burden… nothing more than animals that served the Humans.

I was sick at the sight… physically sick, but there was nothing I could do… not at that moment. I am just happy that Pandorica and the rest of them were safe.

Finally, I made it to the steps of the temple. I was hungry and exhausted, so I sat down and my "friend" ran off to get me some food. I will rest a little and then check out the building. Until then I just hope whatever I have to do works.

I spent the day looking around. The closer I got to one building in the center of town, the warmer the sword got. If I remember correctly, yet with everything I had experienced I couldn't be sure of anything anymore, but this time I was... it was the old building where the Zartoon leaders met. The doors were open and there were no guards, so I went over and started climbing the steps.

"What are you doing there?" a voice asked from behind me. "This building is for historians only."

I knew that I had to think quickly and make whatever I said believable. "I am a historian," I said as I turned to find an old man facing me.

The man looked at me. "I have never seen you before," he said.

"I have been at a temple a couple days from here," I said. "There is a community of Zartoon and Humans who live there, and they have records there, going back more than two thousand generations."

"Two thousand generations?" he asked with a confused and doubtful tone in his voice.

"Yeah," I replied. "Two thousand generations. It is a complete history of the families, the wars they have fought, and how the community started and flourished. It was very interesting. I was just going to compare the records here to see if they have any connection to the settlers at the temple." He must have believed me because he not only allowed me entry… he also escorted me through the door.

"The records you are looking for are down that way," he said as he pointed to a door at the end of the hall. "I have to leave, but I am sure you will find everything you need." He turned and walked back out of the building, leaving me all alone.

The sword was not only burning hot, but it was vibrating. I was close to whatever I was supposed to do, but I still don't know what that is.

ENTRY 70
21.05.63.11.45


I have been hiding for the last few hours until everyone was gone. I could hear people outside, but the building itself was completely empty. The sword was so hot that I could feel my skin starting to burn through the cloth. I wish I knew what this thing was doing... what was going to happen when I did whatever it was I am supposed to do! Right now though I am letting the sword and fate lead me, so that I can find out exactly what it is I have to do.

Now, at the end of this long hallway, I saw something on a pedestal. It was glowing. I took the white sword out of my bag and I saw that it was glowing the same color as the pedestal. Suddenly I knew what I was supposed to do.

I walked slowly down the hall, but it didn't take me as long as it should have, the pedestal was about nine feet tall with Zartoon writing all over it. By now, I was starting to be able to read the language. It contained, in brief, the complete history of the Zartoon people... not only their history but also their religion and philosophy. I read as much as I could. To tell the truth, it was quite amazing. Even though I had learnt so much from Pandorica, about her people, but that was nothing compared to what was written here. I suddenly felt no longer frustrated about what I had to do, now I knew I had to save the

Zartoon and the hybrids and their families.

There were also instructions among the writings. "The white sword is the most powerful of all Zartoon artifacts," it said. "Only one person, the chosen one, may harness its power and they will be the savior of the Zartoon at their time of direst need."

As soon as I finished reading, a small slot opened about a foot or two above me. It was the same size as the blade of the sword, and the light emanating from it was pulsating faster and faster.

I raised the sword. I hesitated for a second, not knowing what was going to happen, but once again, I knew I had to do it, and that I was destined to do this.

"You must," a Zartoon voice said from behind me. "You must use the sword!"

I looked and there was a Zartoon priest standing about a foot behind me... rather, his image was standing behind me. "This history has gone on too long. It is time for it to end and another to begin."

I didn't understand what he meant, but I was listening.

"Too many souls have been lost in useless conflict, you, Fa Nex, have been chosen as the one being who could put an end to it."

Somehow I knew that he was willing me to do so, so I took the sword and shoved it as hard as I could into the slot. Between the intense light and a sound that would have deafened any mortal, I could barely keep from passing out, but I did drop to my knees and I felt blood dripping from my mouth, nose and eyes.

Once the light and the sound stopped I rose to my feet. The man was still there looking at me. "You have the courage of your fathers," he said. "Now, go, and face your new world."

I walked down the hall and out of the building. It was amazing. The sun was shining, and there were hundreds of people standing in front of the building. They weren't walking around and they weren't talking... they were just looking at me.

I could feel the spirit of that aged Zartoon when I started to speak. "This is a Zartoon city," I started. "You will leave the city and return to your own homes. This war that you have been fighting is over as of now. You WILL live together and that is my law and beyond contestation. Do you all understand?"

There was a murmur through the crowd, but no one argued. They all walked away with some of their belongings and within an hour... they were all gone from the city.

Pandorica showed up about a half an hour later, and as soon as she saw what had happened, she just disappeared without even giving me a hug, a kiss, or anything. She must have rushed back to tell her family and the Council, I do not know. I searched for her, but I certainly could not find her.

However, when I took a second look, the

city was totally empty. Even the Zartoon I had seen being used as beasts of burden had disappeared, it was as if as if they were never there. Maybe they have all rushed back to their Zartoon families to tell them of the news. So now, I do not expect anyone to be here for a couple of days, so I have time to relax and enjoy the peace and quiet for a while, and get some much needed sleep.

ENTRY 71
23.05.63.13.10


I woke up today feeling so much more relaxed, I thought about all that had happened, and realized that Pandorica would never have just disappeared, maybe her presence had just been an illusion, just like the ancient Zartoon who had spoken to me by the pedestal.

So I immediately rushed back into the forest to get Pandorica, knowing now all was safe for her to be able to return to the city with me.

Of course, having left her alone in the woods for so long, being a female, she didn't understand any of this, so I got slapped on the shoulder more than once and called every name she could think of. A lot of them were in the Zartoon language, but from the tone of her voice, I could tell that it sure wasn't good.

After I told her all that had happened, it didn't take her long to calm down and we kissed and made up, she told me how proud of me she was, and then hand in hand we walked back into the empty city together

Soon after our return, many Zartoon families arrived to reclaim their homes and businesses. Then Pandorica's family arrived a couple of hours later. It was such a happy celebration, with the Zartoon reclaiming their homes and shops. Some came up, hugged me, and thanked me for allowing their people to return to their lands. I accepted their thanks, and then I noticed something really strange. I was the only Human in the city.

"Where are the Humans?" I asked a couple of the elders.

"When you used the sword and wished that the Humans would return to their city...," one of the elders said. "... All the Humans who lived with us also had to return to their own kind."

"I did not want that," I said in shock. "I just wanted to liberate the city for you."

"We are grateful for that," he said. "We will recover from losing our loved ones... we always do." Then my thoughts went to Rhosly... "What happened to the Hybrids?" I asked/ The elder was reluctant to answer until I pressed him.

"They are not welcome, neither here nor in the Human city. They have to wander the desert until they find somewhere to settle away from us all."

"But Rhosly helped me get your city back," I said now I was getting really angry.

"That does not matter," he said as he started to turn from me. "She is gone!"

I was freaking furious when Pandorica came up to me and asked me what was wrong. I explained it to her and then I asked her a question. "Why am I still here?" I asked. She gave me some airy fairy bull reply, that I was linked to the sword, but I knew it wasn't true but I wasn't going to push it. I was going to try and find a way to fix all of this

I thought for quite a while as to what I should do. Not one of the Zartoon elders offered any ideas. Needless to say, I am frustrated so badly that it is bordering on rage, but I am trying my best to keep my cool. Pandorica has been beside me the entire time. I know that I lost my composure with her a while back, but I do love her, and I know that she realizes this.

"I have to undo what I did," I said as an idea flashed into my head. I didn't wait for Pandorica to answer me... I just took off running to the pillar that held the white sword. Pandorica was soon just behind me, but she let me be and didn't say a word

It was only a few minutes before I entered the building and walked up to the pedestal. The sword was still there and it was still glowing, as was the slot where I had placed it. "You know you are son of a bitch," I said not expecting a reply. "If I would have known I would have thrown you in the water back at the falls and never ever brought you this far."

"Fa Nex," Pandorica said. "What are you planning?"

"Something I know I have to do," I replied.

"Fa Nex, no," she said in a very strong tone.

"I have to," I said in a tone that was as serious as hers. As I spoke, I reached up, grabbed the sword and pulled it out of the pillar. Immediately the ground began to violently shake, tiles fell from the ceiling, and the walls of the building cracked as they tried to stay upright. The sword was still in my hand. It began glowing brighter than even the sun, and I could feel my skin being burned from my hand.

Then, suddenly, everything stopped. The shaking, the light and the heat were all gone. The sword was back to the way it was when I first saw it... then it crumbled into dust as it fell through my fingers and onto the floor.

"Oh Fa Nex my husband, what have you done!" Pandorica screamed. I didn't have the chance to answer before the two soldiers grabbed me, threw me down and hog tied me. Pandorica tried to fight them off, but they threw her down as I was picked up and carried out. The next thing I knew was that I was in a cell beneath one of the buildings...

ENTRY 73
25.05.63.10.54

I have been here for two days. I have not had the chance to talk to anyone. They have even kept Pandorica away from me. I guess I am lucky, they let me keep my notes and pad so I can still record what is happening. I do not even know why they are holding me except that maybe they are very angered that I destroyed the sword...

I just got done eating breakfast. They brought me some kind of egg and meat. I have no idea what it was and I didn't care. With what they are feeding me, I am lucky I am still okay. I am trying to keep as fit as I can... mainly of course pacing around my cell, and that is, I must say, getting rather boring. I wouldn't care if they brought someone in to keep me company, but I sure don't see that happening anytime soon.

You know... I have heard some noises in the last couple of days. They sounded like explosions, but it is hard to tell. God, I wish I knew what was happening. I was thinking maybe the Humans were attacking the Zartoon, trying to get the city back. I hope that, isn't it, but I don't know. I am isolated and I know nothing.

There is someone coming, so I had better stop for now. I will write more once I find out what is going on.

## ENTRY 74
### 27.05.63.09.05

I was awakened at dawn and taken to a chamber in building above me. There, sitting in judgement, were the Zartoon elders. Amongst them are certainly more than a few who were so happy to see me when I first came to the city. Back then, they always greeted me as a good friend, and I was generally treated with great respect as if I was almost royalty. Now they look at me, as if they didn't even know me.

There was a Zartoon female standing beside me. She told me that I was being charged with the destruction of a very important artifact. "The white sword was irreplaceable," she said. "It was the one thing that united the Zartoon people into one, and it was the one thing that could protect the Zartoon from the Humans. Fa Nex you have betrayed us, by destroying the sword by removing it from the pedestal."

"I did it so that all your children could come home," I said. "Isn't that what the parents here wanted?"

"Not at the cost of losing the sword," she replied. She was angry, but even so I figured out that she was here to defend me. I didn't see how she was going to do that since she believed that I had committed a crime against her people.

The "trial" came to order. I had to stand there as the charges were read in Zartoon. I couldn't quite understand everything that they were saying, but they made it sound as if I had destroyed all of Zartoon. They called a couple witnesses… which even included Pandorica, who was no help to them whatsoever, as she insisted on repeating all the good I had done. All this went on and on for more than three hours before my "lawyer" got up and ordered the doors to the chamber opened.

"We demand to speak," a voice cried out from a crowd that rushed through the door and down the aisle. "We demand to speak," the voice shouted again.

"Honored elders," my lawyer said. "These are the half breeds who had been banned from the city because of the sword. They are innocents who have done nothing other than be born of two loving parents. They do not deserve what the sword did to them. They have always been part of our society, and they always should be." At that moment, the entire chamber erupted into cheers, and I swear that I saw some of the elders even crying with remorse.

After all this, the elders left the room. It felt like an eternity before they came back, but when they did the entire chamber went silent. "Fa Nex," the elder in the center said as he sat down. "You are guilty of the crime of destroying the white sword… that is a fact, but it is also a fact that you did what you did to protect a new generation of the Zartoon race. That, we all agree, should be commended, but we also agree we cannot let you go unpunished."

The crowd was getting extremely restless as the elder paused before announcing the sentence.

"Fa Nex, the punishment for destroying such an item is death, but we are not going to do that," the elder said. "You will be banished from all contact with any Zartoon for a period of one month. During that time you may do as you wish, just not within the city walls, or have any contact with the Zartoon."

I knew what that meant. In the olden days, American Indians would banish their people who did wrong, hoping that they would die in exile. I had to leave... that seemed the better of the two options... but I also knew I would survive. I knew where to go and what to do.

ENTRY 75
30.05.63.14.20 5


It has been three days since I was evicted from the Zartoon city. I miss Pandorica terribly, we did not even have a chance to hold each other before I left. All I saw was her face, she was sitting with her family, and she was crying. I walked a great deal in these last three days, I tried going to the Human city, but I was fired upon as I approached the walls. Then I remembered something. I did know a safe haven... that temple where I got the white sword. They thought well of me, and treated me with more respect than I deserved, so I headed there.

I arrived here this morning. When I looked, I did not recognize what I was looking at. The people who used to live together in peace, sharing shelters, food and reveling in their existence had changed. Humans, Zartoons and Hybrids were living in separate camps. They were still close together, but they were all still separate. I watched as a Human and a Zartoon came out from, if I remember right, the breeding lodge. Each was carrying a baby. They weren't Human or Zartoon young... they were Hybrid babies. It shocked me, but they took each of the young and walked them into the cavern I had found. Shortly after they emerged without the babies.

"What is going on," I screamed. "Where are those babies?"

"Our god has told us that those born of Human and Zartoon are cursed and must be destroyed," one of the nurses said as I grabbed her by the arm.

"Who is this god?" I asked. I was furious, and I didn't care if she knew it or not.

"Fa Nex... the keeper of the white sword," she said as she looked into the heavens. "Our elder tells us the words that our god Fa Nex sends for us to follow."

I was angry, angrier than I have ever been. "Where is this elder who can speak with your god?" I asked. She pointed to the cavern and said that he lived within the ground. Before I left to see him, I told her, "I will let you know... I am Fa Nex and if you kill one more child, I will bring my wrath upon you and everyone around you."

I don't know if she believed me or not, but her face went pale and she ran into the breeding lodge and, within seconds, she and several other nurses were making their way into the cavern to retrieve the babies.

I went into the cavern shortly after they did. "Where is he?" I screamed. "I want him and I want him right now!"

An old man came out from behind one of the large rocks that lined the wall. He must have been at least eighty years old if he was a day. "I am who you seek," he said. His eyes were clear and I had a feeling that his wit was as sharp as a razor.

"Do you know who I am?" I asked as I watched every move the man made. He said that no, he had no idea who I was, so I reminded him. "I am Fa Nex and you are using my name to commit infanticide."

"If you are Fa Nex, which I doubt, I have only been doing your work," he said.

"You have not done my work," I shouted angrily, as I grabbed him and violently shook him. "I would never order segregation and the murder of innocents." I had such an urge to grab a rock and beat this old man to death, but luckily common sense prevailed, and I fought the urge. Instead, I threw him against the wall, tore a piece of cloth from his clothing and tied him up.

I grabbed his arm and we walked through the bodies of hundreds of Hybrid babies as we left the cavern. Once we got outside, I yelled for everyone - Human, Zartoon, and Hybrid, to gather at the foot of the stairs. "You may or may not know me," I said to the crowd. "I am Fa Nex. I have returned from a long journey, and I am ashamed by what I see." A lot of the people knew who I was, and they spread the word quickly that their god had returned. "This man has caused strife and murdered in my name. He never spoke for me. I would not allow such things to ever happen. From this moment, all citizens will revert to the way things were…

this I command. Hybrid babies will no longer be killed. They will be raised by their parents and that is beyond contestation.

One last thing, before I give this man to you for you to punish as you see fit. Every baby in this cavern will be given a respectable funeral. They have done nothing to deserve their deaths, and they will be given the respect they deserve... that is my command."

This started happening immediately. I know that it will take time, but at least it is a start back to harmony and life.

ENTRY 76
31.05.63.17.03


Honestly, I do not know how much of this I can take. I haven't seen or heard anything about Pandorica in days. I have no idea if she is alive, or dead, or if they are doing some bad things to her because of her marriage to me. I sent a couple of the Zartoon to the city early this morning. They were more than happy to go, since I stopped all of the trouble here. It will be the day after tomorrow before they return. Until then, I just have to wait.

I had a good day today, though. I performed ten weddings... some Human, some Zartoon and some of Hybrid couples. I liked those the best. I also got to bless three babies who were born today, they were so beautiful that I just had to smile.

This is going to be an extremely short entry today. I just wanted to record what was happening and how I felt. I hope the days will always be just as good. If only Pandorica was here to share this, I know she would be pleased, I miss her so. Oh well... Until next time...

ENTRY 77
02.06.63.20.36

I have been here a couple of days now. Everything is peaceful, so I decided to do some exploring. Earlier this morning I walked about ten miles from the village, and I found a crack in the side of one of the stone mountains that surrounded the area. It looked really big and really deep. Of course, I had to check it out to see what I could find.

I went back and got a torch from the village, and once I started to leave again, a young Zartoon boy decided that he wanted to go with me, and there was no way I was going to talk him out of it. "What is your name, boy?" I asked.

"My name is Vesisku," he replied. "I know this area like the back of my hand. I've wandered around here ever since I was a baby." Then he smiled and said something very, very interesting. "I know where something is that you have to see." Now that's definitely piqued my interest, so I let him not only come with me, I let him lead the way.

It was amazing! It was almost as if he was reading my mind. We made it back to the crack I had found earlier. "It is in there," he said as he pointed at the opening.

"What's in there?" I asked, but instead of answering, he took me by the wrist and led me inside. This path was not made by any living being. It was purely natural, and it was very dangerous, to say the least. I could see dust falling from the ceiling with every step we took and, between the creaking of moving rocks and the sounds of giant rocks falling to the ground, echoes filled the air so badly that you could feel them throughout our bodies. Still, we continued into the bowels of the planet.

The torch we had really wasn't helping much, except when we found a chamber about two hundred yards from the opening, and then we found out what a curse that torch could be. Inside that chamber were hundreds, maybe thousands of very large bats, and the flickering light of the torch woke them up and started them flying around us... and believe me they weren't happy!

As we tried rushing through, they came down from the ceiling and started buzzing our heads. Their wings beat on us so badly that it was hard to stay conscious.

The cavern was full of green light from the self-iridescence on the chests and stomachs of the bats, and the sounds of the animal's sonar. I guess there are some things that are the same across the universe... the saying "blind as a bat" still has meaning.

By the time we made it across the chamber, my body was extremely bruised, and I had quite a few deep cuts in my arms from where I tried chasing the bats away from us. I am sure that I was bitten at least a dozen times. The bites were gushing blood, and each tooth mark felt as if my skin was on fire. Vesisku was a lot calmer than I was. He was bitten, bruised and beaten the same as me, but he knew something, that I didn't.

"Fa Nex," he started. "Find a rock and sit on it fast." I didn't ask why, I just did as he said. "Now relax Fa Nex," he said as he settled onto a big flat rock and then I saw him get weaker and finally pass out. It wasn't long before I felt the same way, and I fell into a deep sleep.

During my sleep I saw so many different worlds. Each one was more spectacular than the one before. I was truly in paradise. I saw music and heard colors in my travels, and I swear that I was riding a big purple unicorn. But, just before I woke, I saw visions of Earth and the home I left.

I knew one thing... I had better write this before I forgot everything that happened. I will record more later tomorrow.

ENTRY 78
03.06.63.13.08


I don't know what that was last night. I saw so many things that I will never understand and, to be honest, I don't think that I would ever want to again. The thing is, today is a new day, so I want to see what is hiding down the cave a ways down.

Vesisku was well awake, long before I started to stir, so he had breakfast done waiting for me. Amazingly, he had made what appeared to be some kind of Zartoon pancakes and some kind of meat. I knew that they didn't have bacon on Zartoon but, it sure tasted like bacon, smelled like bacon and looked like bacon, so to me, it was bacon. I was starving, so it didn't matter what it was, I was going to eat all of it I could. It took us about an hour to eat and get ready to start out again and another couple of hours to get to where we were going.

There were several "obstacles" as we walked deeper and deeper into the ground. The worst was a two hundred foot drop into total darkness. It was nearly vertical and, although there were some ropes hanging down the side, the way I figured they were already ancient when the planet was new. I was not going to allow Vesisku to climb down using them and I sure as hell wasn't going to use one. "My mama didn't raise her no fool," as my uncle would say. But, then again, she might have, because I didn't wait. I just walked over to the edge and jumped into the chasm, followed closely by the boy.

It took what seemed to be a very long time that we were falling, before we hit bottom. Now, I know that no one who reads this is going to believe it, but when we finally hit the floor, we were able to simply stand up and walk away. The floor was covered by a thick layer of moss, and under that was a pool of flowing water, so we landed as gently as if we were caught in our mother's loving arms.

I could see four passages leading from the room where we were standing. "Well, which way do we go?" I asked.

"Fa Nex," Vesisku stated, with slight fear in his voice, "I have been to the edge of that cliff, but never any further. To tell the truth, Fa Nex, I was actually too scared to go on."

I'll tell you… I just couldn't be angry at the boy. He was just a boy after all, so he shouldn't be expected to be as brave as a full-grown man. Yet, it was also obvious, he did have guts, when he needed them. He'd proven that to me by jumping when I did, and not knowing how that jump it was going to come out."

Since he didn't know, and I certainly didn't know, I decided to let either fate or luck tell me where to go. It would probably be the best idea to just flip a coin a couple of times to decide which way to go. It came up a head and then a tail, so that told me that the third passage would be the way to go.

It led about ten more miles into the rock. There were cliffs along the way. Nothing like the one we had come down earlier. They were no more than maybe twenty feet or so, and some had waterfalls that we floated down, and others had updrafts that kept us from falling too fast. Considering what we had gone through earlier, that part of the trip was indeed fun.

At the end of the long passage, I walked into a rotted wooden door. The logs were thick and covered with rough grey bark. Yes, my eyes had become so adapted to the dark, that I could even see dull levels of color, and I could definitely see that the door was grey and the rocks were a lighter grey. But, as I was saying, the logs were rotten and they fell apart when I touched them. It took me about an hour, but I was able to tear the wood apart and cut an opening for Vesisku and I to make it through.

Once inside the room, it was as if we had stepped through the rocks and back into the outside. The light was as bright as the sun. The air was cool and moist, and there was a breeze that was so gentle you could miss it if you weren't looking for it.

The walls were silver metal with twelve stone pillars at equal distances around the room, and each pillar had a silver and gold soldier standing before it looking at two big stone boxes in the center of the room. Each of the boxes had engraving on all four sides, as well as very ornate lids. On a large plaque on each of the boxes were what I could only assume were names. One read Adm and the other said Kisikillillake.

You know there are just some things that you know you shouldn't do, but you do it anyway. Well, I decided that I would open the two boxes and see what was inside. Even with Vesisku helping, it took all of our strengths combined to move the lids over the sides.

When we got them open we looked inside and saw two bodies... one male and one female. The female was Zartoon while the male was Human. In the Human's hand was a scroll made out of some kind of thin animal skin. It was written in Zartoon, but it was an old dialect so I couldn't read it, and even Vesisku was having trouble, so I decided that we should just find a corner of the chamber and rest, then figure out what it says tomorrow so that is just what we did. I just hope I can get some sleep.

Vesisku's eyes lit up a couple of hours ago. "I can read this," he said. "It is an ancient dialect, but it is still close enough that I can make out what is being said.

"Well?" I asked as I jumped up off of a rock and stood in front of him. He started to answer, but before he could, I looked more carefully at the writing. I could read some of it, but not much so I needed him. "What does it say?"

"I cannot believe it," he said. He was smiling, but there was a look of shock in his eyes. "There is a legend on Zartoon, It is part of our religion, but no one ever really believed it."

"A legend," I said. I was kind of puzzled, somewhat scared and confused but I really wanted to know.

"The story is that one of our gods set forth to make a species to live on this planet. They made a pair of creatures to bring life to Zartoon. Their names were Adm and Kiskillilleke. I think that we may have found their tomb." Then his look changed as he went over to another pillar. "By the gods!!!," he said.

"What... what did you find," I asked as I rushed over to him. He looked at me. I could not tell what he was thinking, or even what he was going to say, but whatever it was it shocked him.

"Adm was Zartoon," he said. "He was the first Zartoon and the father of us all!" Then he stopped for a full five minutes before he continued. "Kiskillilleke...she was Human! It says here that they produced many children. The ones who had the Zartoon look stayed on this planet. The ones who looked like Kiskillilleke left the planet after several generations. It says that they traveled to the third planet of this star."

"Earth," I asked. "They traveled to Earth."

"If that is what you call that blue dot of light," he said. "Yes, they traveled to Earth."

I dropped to the ground. I don't remember if I was looking for a sign from God or what, but I just knew that I wasn't able to stand. I was looking at the graves of Adam and Eve... the beings God created when the Earth was new. Once I got to my feet, I ran over to the two tombs. I knew that I shouldn't do what I was thinking of doing, but honestly, I don't think I had a choice! I was standing next to Kiskillilleke's sarcophagus when Vesisku joined me.

I didn't have to say anything. It was as if he could read my mind. We both put our hands on the lid and slid it slowly away from us. One we could see inside we saw the most beautiful Human female ever. Her hair was a pure gold blonde and her body was flawless. Even after so many millions of years, she was perfect. Inside the other coffin was the body of a young Zartoon. He was not a warrior or anything like that. He was as beautiful as the female's body. *My God,* I thought. *I am looking at the true beginning of life.* I didn't know what to do next so Vesisku and I settled down for the night. Tomorrow I will know what to do, but tonight my head was swirling just a little too much to think.

## ENTRY 80
04.06.63.11.01


    I had one hell of a time sleeping last night. It wasn't that I was in a crypt. That didn't bother me in the least, but my mind kept going back to the writing on the walls. No one should have that knowledge. So many billions of people spent their lives believing that god created man as the only beings in the universe and now I am only one of two who know the truth. Life began on Zartoon and moved to Earth from here. Then, another thought came to me... if this was true, there are no purebred Humans or Zartoons. Every being in the solar system was a mixture of Zartoon and Human.

    "Are you ready to leave?" Vesisku asked as he rose from his sleep.

    I told him I wasn't quite ready. "I want to spend another day here," I said. I wanted to have him translate more of the carvings, and explain what they meant, and maybe who wrote them.

    After breakfast, we went over to a wall that was covered from top to bottom in an alphabet that resembled the cuneiform lettering of the ancient Sumerians. I only knew that from seeing it in books, but it was easy to recognize. Vesisku said that it was the story of Kiskillilleke and Adm. It was written by their eldest son Teresku.

    "Kiskillilleke and Adm were born of the god. They were granted with immortality and the power to procreate to spread the image of him across the planet," it said. "They were given life in order to bring a desolate planet forth with intelligent, and peaceful life. They lived for more than 3000 cycles of the moons and gave birth to more than 10,000 children. Some appeared with smooth skin while some appeared differently. This caused a rift between the children, and the first fighting began.

Because Kiskillilleke and Adm could not keep peace between their children, their immortality was taken, and the god allowed them to be the first of many deaths from the battles. The fighting lasted for 100 cycles of the moons and, when it was over, I entombed my parents in this crypt in the hope that their dream for a peaceful world could someday be realized.

However, the god was not finished. He banished the smooth skins to a distant planet and barred them from knowing of the Zartoon people, until a time when the two peoples could once again coexist in peace."

"Well, that never happened," I said.

Vesisku smiled and told me that indeed there was one time, not long before where Zartoon and Humans did live in peace. "Then someone said something, and someone else said something else, and the fighting started again," he said. "Now, I do not believe that it can be fixed. The hatred is just too much."

I thought that it wasn't hard to stop the fighting in the small community above, so maybe, just maybe I could get it to work on a global scale. I would just have to get Humans and Zartoon together and show them what I have seen in this tomb. How could they continue fighting after hearing such a message and that they were really as one?

ENTRY 81
04.06.63.22.58


I have to have time to think... to figure out what to do. I decided to send Vesisku out and back to town. He had to send out messages to each and every settlement, town and city, both Human and Zartoon, and tell them to send a representative to the mouth of this cave. This will be a totally, completely neutral site and hostilities would not be accepted. This had to be what I had to do. I had to get the word out. "Tell them that the gods have ordered this meeting."

"What about you?" Vesisku asked.

"I am going to stay here and learn as much as I can," I said. "You just make sure that all chosen are here in seven days."

"May I ask why?" Vesisku asked.

"I am going to put an end to all of this, one way or the other." I was maybe sounding a little too stern as I spoke to him. I mean after all he had done nothing but help me the entire time I have been here. "Please do as I ask," I said in as pleasant a voice as I could. He agreed. Then he turned and left the cave.

As soon as he left, I started reading again. I couldn't understand a lot, but every second I stood there I was able to understand more and more of the wall carvings. I had read one panel when I realized one thing... Vesisku had taken all of the food and water with him. I'm left with just a blanket and that is all. I tried calling out to him, but all I could hear the echo of my voice coming back down the tunnels. I was alone, hungry, and tired, but I had to do this no matter what, then, as if things weren't bad enough, my damn light died.

I settled down next to the caskets. I wanted to think and think hard when I saw something I could not believe. The cave was filled with light. I could not see where it was coming from, but I knew it wasn't from outside. As my eyes adjusted, I saw where it was coming from... it was the engravings. They were casting a faint light. Singly, it wasn't enough to see with, but when all of the walls, the ceiling and even the caskets started glowing there was more than enough light.

With all that happened, it was time to rest so I curled up on the floor. Tomorrow may be a better day.

ENTRY 82
07.06.63.14.10


It has been three days since Vesisku left. I have spent the entire time studying and memorizing every word and every philosophy on the walls. It is all truly amazing. Everything we learned about life on Earth from the creation and all the way through history was written here. It is all the same message except that it was written about here and the Zartoon.

It teaches that all beings are the same whether they are Zartoon, Human, all the way down to the swamp slime I saw along the shores of the waterways. Everyone is the same and should be treated as brothers and sisters.

I thought back to the way the settlement above was before things changed. They had no idea, but they were living life the way that was ordained for them at the beginning of time. I had to get that back for the whole planet.

Vesisku walked in about five minutes ago. He had done as I instructed. Representatives of every city, village and settlement on the planet were waiting up at the entrance and I knew that I had to deliver the message I had learned.

"They are here," Vesisku said as he stepped beside me.

"Tell them to wait," I said. "I am hoping that they will talk between themselves while they wait." Vesisku did as he was told and, even all the way in the tunnel, I could hear discussions taking place. Yes, there were arguments, but from what I could hear, there was no fighting. That was a good thing.

I did make them wait for a few hours. I don't know how many, but finally I walked up the steps. I was all alone and my stomach was turning. During the last few steps I thought about turning back. I could end this planet if I said the wrong thing.

Finally, I stepped through the door and I saw hundreds of Humans and Zartoon standing before me. Each group was carrying a banner of their own lands. "Lower those banners," I yelled. "You are all one people of one set of parents and one god. This fighting between the Humans and Zartoon will stop now."

"Why should we listen to you?" someone yelled from the crowd. "We do not know who you are."

"I do understand that you have no idea who I am," I said. Then I said that I wanted the Zartoon and the Humans to select one of each to accompany me into the tunnel. "I want you to see what I have seen, learn what I have learned." It took a considerable while, but two were finally selected. As they walked up the steps, I saw that they were wearing robes that would be considered elegant by any royalty on Earth. Anyway, they stood beside me, shook hands, and then we walked into the tunnel.

I spoke to them all of way the down to the

tomb. I pointed out how many similarities they had and how the differences were so small that they should not cause such hatred. Finally, as we entered the tomb, the two of them agreed that there shouldn't be such hatred between the two groups.

"What is this place?" one of the two asked as we stepped through the opening.

"This is the tomb of Adam and Kiskillilleke... the parents of both Humans and Zartoon," I said. "The words in this room tell you how life is to be lived. The racism between the two groups has to stop now... it is the law from your creator."

We stood there for an hour as they read the carvings and talked between themselves. It was more than a few minutes after they stopped talking when they insisted on going back to the surface. I agreed.

The walk wasn't that long... only a couple of minutes before we stepped into the sunlight. Both representatives raised their hands to silence the crowd.

"You will listen to this man," one of them said. "He has the words of the creator and everyone will listen and obey."

I stepped between them, but before I could say a word I saw a flash from the back of the group and a loud rumbling sound. The next thing I knew, something hit me in the chest. It was hot and painful and, as it hit, I felt my mind fade and the world around me turned to black...

ENTRY 83
07.06.63.16.10 3

I had no idea what happened. I just remember that I had a burning pain in my chest. I thought for sure that I was dead, but my eyes opened and the first thing I saw was a beautiful young woman. She had light blonde hair with golden streaks and eyes the color of a country.

"I see that you are awake," she said with a smile on her face. "You have been asleep a long time haven't you?"

It took a few second for my mind to focus before I answered. "I don't know... have I?"

"Well, I have been here for three days and this is the first time I have seen your eyes so I guess it has been a long time," she said with a smile.

"Now, the important question," I asked as her eyes opened wide. "Where am I?"

She laughed loudly, which made me feel a bit better. "Sweetie, you are in Portland, Maine," she said as she took my hand. I kind of went into shock, but that was just for a second. "You are in the Portland Community Hospital. They brought you in with a strange burn on your chest and you were wearing the strangest clothes. I looked over to the closet and saw the clothes I was wearing moments before.

I was still confused, but then I asked one more important question. "Where is Pandorica?"

I asked with some hope.

"Well, my name is Pandora," she said as she smiled again. "I guess you may have heard it spoken here and misunderstood what they were saying." I started crying, almost beyond control. By the time the last tear rolled down my face, she gave me a kiss on the cheek.

"It will all be okay," she whispered softly in my ear.

Somehow I knew it would be so I went to sleep still holding her hand.

## EPILOGUE

That was over 20 years ago. I ended up marrying Pandora and we had two children… a boy and a girl. I named the girl Rosealee and, the boy, well, I named him after my first son. He is Bledri Williams II.

Sometimes at night, Pandora and I sit out in the yard. I point to the red planet that floats across the sky. I tell her of Zartoon, Pandorica and all of the others I met as well as the adventures I had there… I doubt that she believes me, but she enjoys hearing the stories.

So often I wonder, was I part of Zartoon's history or was I part of its future? I do know, and possibly I never will. But, the most important thing is that I remember everything I learned there, and I still spread the words of Fa Nex wherever I go. I just hope one day it will make a difference and we will all live in harmony, we the children of Adm and Kiskillilleke.